To Kevin,
my wayward boy in all the right ways

Nothing is far and nothing is near, if one desires. . . . There is only one big thing—desire.

—Willa Cather, *The Song of the Lark*

Contents

꘎ ✦ ꘎

CONTENTS (*continued*)

II. FAR

Acknowledgments

⋘ ✦ ⋙

I OWE MOUNTAINS to everyone at WVU Press, especially Derek Krissoff who guided me through the past several months with wisdom, support, and perfect intuition. Sara Georgi has had my back throughout the editing of this book. I'm beyond grateful for her insightful comments, close reading, attention to detail, and our shared love of the backcountry. Many thanks to Abby Freeland for helping me negotiate the topography of publishing. Than Saffel—your vision is magic. I'm so appreciative of your work.

Thank you to Elon University for its generous support and funding over several years. Thank you to the Weymouth Center for providing me with space to work when I needed it. I'm grateful to the editors and judges who selected "A Portrait of My Father in Three Places" for a Pushcart nomination, "No More to the Lake" as a *Best American Essays* notable, and "On Not Marrying a Ranger" for first place in the Notes from the Field contest.

Over many years, my writing group has read drafts of these essays and many others. I'm indebted to Barbara Gordon, Megan Isaac, and Janet Myers (and past member Janet Warman) for their intelligence, insight, and support.

I feel gratitude to so many for their help with parts or all of this book, including Julie Averette, Lynne Bisko, Karen Bjork, Mark Brewin, Don Eron, Mary Jo Festle, Jessica Keough, Carl Klaus, Susan Lohafer, John Price, Patrick Rudd, Carol de St. Victor, and Ned Stuckey-French. Special thanks to Liz Clift and Jeremy Jones for pointing me to opportunities I would have missed. Many thanks to Dan Roche for reading the manuscript right when I needed it. And super special thanks to Kay Young who called me her Lady Thoreau from the beginning and didn't mean it as a joke.

It takes a good hiking group for me to keep things balanced. I'm indebted to Brenda Bass, Kathleen Conklin, Pat Kato, Julie Overbaugh, and Teresa Rice for allowing me to talk out my work and life on the trail.

I am grateful for the support of so many friends and colleagues, near and far, especially Brian Angell, Kelsey Camacho, Stuart Dischell, Julie Hartman, Luke Johnson, Eliot Meade, Nora Meade, Drew Perry, Ginger Perry, Tita Ramirez, Jeff Saver, James Stramm, and Maureen and Russ Vandermaas-Peeler. Many thanks to Gabie Smith who kept me afloat when our kids were young and still does now that they're grown. Bridget Klauber and E.J. Meade helped me find my way back West; I can't find words for how much I value our friendship. There are no words for how much I miss Bridget.

Thanks to all the Boyles for their generosity, kindness, and love. I lucked out with the lot of you.

Thank you to my father who taught me that it's possible to live an original life. Much love to my amazing mother, Marilyn, and my equally amazing brothers, Scott and Kip, with whom I traveled the terrain of childhood, adolescence, and adulthood. Thank you for allowing me to depict snippets of our lives together.

Many thanks and hugs to Heidi, John, and Kelsey Kircher.

Thank you most of all to my children, Tess Boyle and Luke Boyle, for agreeing to appear in these pages. I have never taken motherhood for granted. You both are bright stars in my sky.

This book is for you, Kevin Boyle. Without your curiosity, generosity, sharpness, and wit, this book would not exist. Thank you for starring in some of these pages. For being my sun.

I. NEAR

A Portrait of My Father
in Three Places

⸺ ✦ ⸺

Wyoming, 1965

I'M TEN the first time my father takes us camping in a national park. Yellowstone, except we're staying next door at Jenny Lake Campground in Teton National Park because my dad likes it better. "Fewer people," he says, even though this campground is full too. My dad has already learned the ropes around here, like how to get a campsite and where to buy ice for the cooler he keeps right outside the tent door. And I like Jenny Lake. Not that I don't like camping in other places, like South Dakota, where we've been before. But this feels like real camping to me. I like how we see herds of wild deer and how it gets so cold at night we have to put on our winter coats just to sit around the campfire.

When it's time for bed that first night, we sleep on air mattresses in flannel sleeping bags. One of my brothers sleeps beside me, and my littlest brother sleeps beside him. I can hear my father sprinkling water on our fire, the hot coals hissing when the water hits them, the smell of smoke all the way in the tent. Then I hear him moving around, making our camp safe and locking the car. When he comes into our home, he unzips the heavy door and stretches out beside my mom. Nothing outside the tent is moving, not even a breeze. I picture the moon somewhere up high.

"Goodnight," my dad says into the perfect square of the tent, and everyone says goodnight right back.

That's when our story happens. Not right then, but an hour or two later, when we all wake up to snoring, and no one says a thing. No one moves, not even my littlest brother. Instead, we lie stiff and dead like logs, listening to a snoring that can't be my father's, but must be something.

"Grizzly?" my mom whispers. My stomach flips, and my father gets ready to protect his family like he's supposed to.

"Don't move," he says. From there everything happens fast. My father slips out of his sleeping bag and steps in the dark toward the door. In his right hand, he is holding something; in his left hand, he is holding something else.

My father says nothing. The bear growls from right outside. A sound like slobber. I close my eyes. I hear the tent unzip. When I do look, I see my father in the doorway facing the bear. He raises one hand and turns on his flashlight; he raises his other hand and pushes down on a big can of OFF! bug spray. Everything is aimed right toward the bear.

The next morning my body feels the lines on the air mattress, and I smell earth and canvas. The sun is gold and awake. Outside I hear the campfire burp and snap, the low voices of my father and mother, and the hollowness of heavy boots on dry, packed dirt as my father checks on something by the picnic table. The air is cold. My brothers' heads are lost in their sleeping bags, and I slip on my jacket and race for my favorite cereal, the kind that comes in little boxes we all three like and fight over and get only for vacations.

When I come out of the tent, breakfast isn't ready, and even from a distance, I can tell our aqua cooler has been through something bad. Its lock is all bent up, and instead of being beside the tent door where I saw it last, it's sitting on the picnic table surrounded by all the food that used to be inside its cold belly: the cheese, eggs, and butter. A carton of milk. They all look different.

"Compliments of our visitor," my father says, and for a moment I imagine our visitor as a furless park ranger coming by after I was asleep.

It takes everything I have to remain calm as I remember what happened—just a few hours ago, in the black of the night, my father was a hero, saving our lives as he greeted the grizzly.

Montana, 1973

I'm eighteen. My dad, my mom, my brothers, and I are on vacation driving across Nebraska and Wyoming in our Ford LTD before making a right-hand turn at Colter Bay and heading up to Glacier National Park. Behind the Ford, we're pulling a wooden pop-up camper, one that is hand built and swerves in the wake of our exhaust like a water-skier. My father has picked it up from the want ads.

My father has picked up a lot of new equipment for this trip: five down sleeping bags, five foam air mattresses, five rectangular backpacks, and a whole fleet of plastic containers recommended—according to my father—by camping experts: a tube for peanut butter, another for mayonnaise, a carton molded to nest half a dozen medium-sized eggs. He buys everything one afternoon from The Backwoods, the only mountaineering store in Omaha. He also purchases an expedition tent in which my youngest brother and I will sleep. The tent features a snow tunnel and a little half-moon panel that can be zipped out of the floor in case you want to light a stove indoors and brew a cup of tea during a blizzard.

"I think," my brother says with a maturity way beyond his twelve years, "that Dad might be feeling his midlife."

I'm not sure about anyone else, but my father seems to be thinking of this vacation as our family's own kind of manifest destiny, our great northern adventure and a step above the Teton National Park area where we have camped for several years. At a gas station south of Flathead Lake, he picks up a copy of *Night of the Grizzlies* for all of us to share during our next two weeks of relaxation. He'd heard of the book back in Omaha, and even though he knows it focuses on two bears that maul two different park visitors in two different areas of Glacier National Park on the same night, he buys it, because he thinks somehow it will help familiarize us with Glacier's topography and emergency procedures—not to mention the park's flora and, especially, its fauna.

After we arrive, the three of us kids register complaints, as if that's our job: "The tent is too small," we say. "The air is too cold." "The sky is too dark." My parents don't respond—just get quiet in a way that's typical. The bottom line is we really don't have much to complain about. It's true that our fluffy sleeping bags aren't rated for Glacier National Park temperatures. It's also true that the trout just aren't biting. But a bigger truth is probably that we are suffering from a case of growing older that keeps us from enjoying a camping trip like this one this particular year. In the past, fly fishing was our number-one activity, and all three of us were always ready to go out as a group and cast by our father's side like shadows. This year he's lucky to have one of us following along for a few minutes. My youngest brother, in what I guess is a show of solidarity with his teenage siblings, even refuses to wear his waders.

Most mornings my father fishes alone, coming back for lunch empty-handed and frustrated. Most afternoons we hike Glacier's trails. By day two when we surprise a grizzly eating huckleberries beside Hidden Lake, all five of us have read through chapter four of the *Night of the Grizzlies*, and my father finally decides to purchase the bells we have seen other hikers wearing. These little back-packing gems warn bears you are present, sort of like a doorbell, but instead of being frugal, my father overbuys and ties several bells to each of our fanny packs so we look and sound like Santa's reindeer, or a small, moving cathedral.

After dinner most evenings, we walk over to the amphitheater and listen to the free campfire programs offered by the park service. It's my father who makes us attend these productions. I'm not sure about my brothers, but I resent sitting on a log looking at slides of tundra and granite when most kids my age are attending rock concerts somewhere. On our fourth night at the amphitheater, I know we're in trouble with a program called something as boring as "Animal Friends of Glacier Park." The ranger in charge—a real go-getter—talks about how he's been fishing a place called Goat Lake on his days off. It's hard hiking to get there, he says, but worth every uphill step. He even recommends using a fly called, for God's sake, the

Yellow Humpy, and he shows us a couple slides of other flies he has wasted valuable time tying. Not two minutes into the program, I notice my father taking notes in the margins of our park map.

When we return to the campsite, my father radiates enthusiasm. "Goat Lake, anyone?" he asks in a happy voice, spreading the map out on the picnic table. In the glow of our Coleman lantern, I follow his index finger over masses of topographical lines up to a tiny blue oval.

"Dad," I say after a few minutes of studying the situation, "Goat Lake is eight miles into the backcountry—it's in Canada."

"It's nothing but a personal theory," my father says, "but I think fishing another country's waters will bring us luck."

In the morning, my father's voice has changed from animated to mute—a pattern so familiar to me I think all fathers stop talking when they are upset or angry and all daughters spend energy worrying about them and trying to get them to smile. As he silently herds us into the car, I realize my father might be something more serious than *a pill*, the term my mother sometimes uses when referring to him. He might, in fact, be a difficult man—a hunch I've been considering for a couple years now, and one that rings true once we arrive at the Goat Lake Trailhead and he retrieves his pole, creel, and backpack from the trunk of the LTD with such speed and purpose I feel as if I'm watching a fast-forward cartoon.

None of us expect what happens next: my father doesn't even say goodbye to his family. Instead he puts himself in high gear and storms up the trail as quickly as a six-foot-three man can storm.

"Dad," I say in a loud enough voice. "Your bear bells . . ."

Not one of us follows. Instead we assess our own situation. The chance of our father returning to the car soon is not good, but it is possible. If we leave to ride horses or drive up the Going-to-the-Sun Road, my father would have a problem: there is no phone at this trailhead, and I don't know who he'd call for a ride if there were. There is not much of anything here, really. Only a couple of parked cars that look dusty and stranded as if someone forgot all about them. I don't get the feeling this place is a hip tourist destination.

My mother is in a bind. At least, that must be what she is thinking now that she is in charge. It's not as if she can sit the three of us down and start up a discussion about her husband's behavior. In the unspoken way our family often communicates, however, we all seem to agree that the best option is to wait for our father right where we are. So that's what we do.

At one point, both my brothers get out their fishing poles and start to cast into a nearby pond. At another point, my mother stretches out in the back seat of the car and naps. There is not a lot of talking. There is no complaining. The sun shines, and there is that quiet that I look for in nature. After lunch, I take a little hike around the area and admire a field of little blue flowers blooming in the shape of bells. When I return, I stop to watch my brothers release a ten-to-twelve-inch brook trout back into the clear water.

At sunset, my father finally comes down the trail, and I can tell, even from a distance, his mood hasn't changed. We all watch him stash his fishing gear into the trunk, take his car keys out of his fishing shorts, and get behind the steering wheel.

"Let's go," he says, and at first, I think he means back to the campground. When we arrive at our site and he begins taking down the expedition backpacking tent and folding up our pop-up camper and making us all break camp, I realize those two words mean something else and that we will miss tonight's campfire program and leave this national park for good.

An hour later, as we drive past Flathead Lake with our pop-up camper behind us, I start wondering about motels. It is ink-black out, and not much traffic is on the two-lane highway. At the next gas station, my mom makes a move to sit in the back seat—to be honest, I think she is tired of being so close to all that dark silence—and I volunteer to sit up beside my dad. I don't ask to drive.

"Dad," I say after another fifty miles, "where are we going?"

"Jenny Lake," he says, surprising me by saying anything at all. "That campground in the Tetons."

"We're camping tonight?" I say.

"Not tonight. It'll be full. We'll be there about dawn, the first car in line for tomorrow."

"We're not sleeping?" I ask, impressed at how well my father has thought everything through.

"Go ahead and sleep," he says.

North of Yellowstone and several hundred miles later, I am still awake. In the back seat, my mother and brothers are not. A wind has come up, and the car careens back and forth in the lane. We're probably going too fast, if rules like that even apply out here on these back roads. My father hasn't talked again for miles. He just stares straight ahead into the blackness, and I do the same.

That's when the buck appears in our headlights. Tall and beautiful, his neck turned with so much grace that he looks like a dancer. His eyes big, shiny globes looking straight at us. In that moment, I think he must be some kind of ghost. But then the LTD crashes into his huge chest, and he folds forward over himself in slow motion, his

head and antlers bowing toward us. And there is sound—
the hollow sound of metal hitting flesh, hitting something
alive—and everyone in the car is awake.

"John!" my mother says.

My father and I get out of the car, we all get out of
the car, and look at the huge dent in the hood. There
is damage, and there are little brown hairs stuck in the
fender at the place where the paint has been disturbed.
There is no buck lying in front of the car—just the space
of where he has been, the space of impact. The car's
engine is still running.

"Maybe he's okay," I say, but I know—we all are old
enough to know—that he isn't, that just beyond the headlights, he is in the biggest trouble ever. I want to suggest
that we help him, but I know we can't, and to say such a
thing out loud would be ridiculous coming from someone
my age. At one point, either my father or mother says the
word *insurance*.

When we get back in the car, my mother takes my
place in the front seat, and everything else is different
too. I'm guessing that everything will stay different, all
the way through Yellowstone National Park to its smaller
cousin, the Tetons, where we will probably be the first in
line at Jenny Lake Campground, just as my father predicts.
A mangled car waiting for the ranger to come on duty, so
we can claim a vacant space, the sun just pushing up into

the sky. Until then we'll drive with nothing but black out the window, my father's hand gripping the steering wheel tightly, trying to keep control.

Colorado, 1982

I'm twenty-seven when my father drives alone across Nebraska to visit me in Rocky Mountain National Park because he's retired now, and my mother is not, and neither of my brothers lives at home. My father bought brand-new hiking clothes for the trip: shorts with pockets, big boots, a lightweight button-down shirt that looks stiff. For the past six years, I have worked in the park as a ranger, and my father has coordinated this visit with my tour of duty at the Lawn Lake Patrol Cabin, 5.2 miles into the backcountry. He has packed in his fly rod, and on the way up the trail I see him eyeing Roaring River for trout. Later, at just the right spot in the clearing, I turn him around, so he can see Longs Peak, the park's only fourteen-thousand-foot mountain, framed—like a faraway surprise—by the aspen, but he doesn't seem interested in dry landscape.

When we arrive at the cabin, my father watches me unbolt the three windows and unlock the padlock on the heavy door as if he can't believe his daughter can do these kinds of things. I don't get the feeling that he thinks me incompetent as much as I sense that these workaday duties aren't part of his master plan for how a daughter of his should turn out. Once we're inside, there are other chores: unpacking the food, airing the bedding, building the fire. My father agrees to get water from the lake, but when I hand him the ten-gallon collapsible plastic jug, I find myself worrying that even the empty receptacle will be too heavy for him. During dinner, my park service radio is on, but it airs mostly static the way it always does when I'm in this drainage. It makes the discomfort I feel with him audible.

"See any trout at the lake?" I say, wondering what other daughters would mention to their sullen father in a twelve-by-twelve-foot backcountry cabin.

"Not really," he says, and I push another log into the stove.

Early the next morning, my father carries his fishing gear out the door slowly, as if his heart hurts, and I go down to the lake with him. The water is slick and clear, not like a mirror as much as a window I can't see through to the bottom. In spite of his interest in trout fishing, my father is a North Woods lake man, and he doesn't seem to admire this high-altitude water. Instead he works at tying on a fly, some kind of streamer—probably one he's been deciding on since we arrived.

I love the cork handle of his fishing pole, the way my father's hand wraps around it as he begins to fish—stopping and starting at first, like an engine trying to get going, and then really beginning to cast, the pole an extension of his long arm as he stretches an arc over the water. For the longest time, I stand there feeling the rhythm of the casting, remembering how I used to mimic him with my own pole, back and forth, admiring the grace of his movements, the concentration in every muscle. What I think about most as I leave him for a short patrol of the four Lawn Lake campsites is my father's intention: to manipulate a fly so that it moves in a way that looks like an insect and not like the simulation that it is. When I return, he has caught one cutthroat, which he's placed in the dark-green backpacking creel he's brought along on this trip. I can't tell whether he's pleased with his catch.

Back when we camped as a family and my father caught all the fish allowed in a single day of fishing, he would clean them and put them on ice in our cooler. I only saw him perform the cleaning ritual once—saw him make a short, sharp cut across the fish's throat with his knife before slicing its underbelly in one long line from tail to jaw. This was when I felt sick, when I saw my father, without a second thought, hold a fish by its mouth with one hand and pull its insides out with his other so that they were visible for anyone to see.

"This is the bloodline," my father said, as he put his hand in the fish's belly again and scraped away a brown and red streak. "All of it comes out." He always left the head on. As far as I know, my father never beheaded a trout—maybe out of respect, maybe because acknowledging a meal's origins seemed most honest to him.

Although I never saw my father clean a fish again, I usually watched him prepare them—watched him roll the fish in flour, salt and pepper them on both sides, and put them in the metal lid of the huge family mess kit that served as our frying pan in the wild. When I was a kid, I didn't eat trout, but I liked smelling them cook, and I liked their brown-gold color against the silver of the pan. My father sautéed them in butter, and even though they looked like works of art when he finished, I don't think my mother liked making them part of her meal. Now, as an adult, I eat trout—not that I fish for them or buy them to prepare myself, not that I forget about how svelte and flashing they look in the wild. But each summer, when my parents visit me in Estes Park, we eat at the Sundeck Restaurant and my mother orders French toast for breakfast while my father and I order Rocky Mountain trout served stiff and whole across our plates.

When my father catches his cutthroat at the Lawn Lake cabin, I expect him to clean it like he used to when I was a child, and I am surprised when instead he goes into the cabin and comes out with the biggest cooking pot he can find before taking it down to the lake and filling it. After that, he transfers the trout from his creel to the silver pot—it barely has room to swim—and carries it up to the cement stoop of the cabin, where he leaves it all afternoon. At dusk I watch my father bring his trout inside with us for the night, like a pet, and I wonder what he plans to feed it.

On our second day out, I'm scheduled to patrol up to Rowe Glacier, and my father decides to stay behind at the lake and fish. Because it's a strenuous hike, I don't try hard to persuade him to come along, but I regret that he'll miss being in a place where the view extends out beyond the tundra to the clouds. As my father prepares his line, tying on a new fly on a new leader, I adjust my daypack before putting my radio in its holster and starting off. It's a day of sun and cloudless sky. Little pink and purple pincushions grow close to the ground at this altitude—and with each step, I feel the tension from the cabin dissolve. When I reach Mummy Pass, I look down and see my father at the east edge of the lake, his arm casting back and forth, as if he is waving to me—except the wave is strange and weak, and as I keep hiking I feel my heart tighten.

On my way back down several hours later, I patrol through the four campsites, but no tents have been pitched, and I have the sense that my father and I are the only people in this landscape. Back at the cabin, I find him sitting on the cement stoop. The air around him smells like pine. Beside him is the cook pot, and when I look down into it, there is not one, but two trout corralled together, side by side and treading water, each eyeing the other from the side of its head.

"Dinner?" I ask, gesturing towards the pot, wondering if my father has been waiting all along to catch two trout before he cleaned one.

"I can't kill them," he finally says, and for a moment I feel a flash of fear, that kind of fear I've felt all my life whenever my father seems vulnerable. Instead of responding, I unzip a side pocket of my pack, get out my water bottle, offer my father a drink, and take a long one myself, thinking it would be easier to be back up at the glacier, eating my dinner alone on a flat rock.

"What are you going to do with the fish?" I ask, wondering if he wants me to clean them, wondering if he wants to release them, wondering if they are, perhaps, even too small to keep. My father says nothing. "I thought you liked trout," I say.

Instead of responding he picks up the cook pot and brings it inside. I watch my father light the Coleman lantern and the Coleman stove—just like he used to light an identical-looking lantern and stove when I was a kid. We have spaghetti and tomato sauce for dinner, and I notice that, in spite of his fishing luck, my father has little energy. For the rest of the evening, he reminds me of a statue, his face chiseled with lines, his brown eyes less bright than ever before.

When I wake on the third day, my father is sitting in a chair by the wood box looking all wrong without a newspaper on his lap. There's rain—I can hear it and smell it, and my father is watching it out the window, thinking about something far away from this cabin. It's hard for me to see him, wherever he's at in the past. I'd rather have him here in the present, talking with the charm and humor he's capable of, or fishing down at the lake, holding the extra loop of line with his left hand, hearing the click, click, click as he slowly winds his reel, trolling his fly on top of the water.

"Are you okay, Dad?" I ask. He hasn't shaved since we've been here, and he looks changed.

My father doesn't even try to tell me how he feels. Instead he asks me what is on my agenda for the day, and I think about all I should be doing to post a sign directing backpackers to their campsite way down at Upper Tileston Meadows: the deep hole I should be digging, the tree I should be felling, the soil I should be tamping down so that the park's message to campers stays up straight and strong.

"With this rain it's hard to say," I answer, thinking I should probably stay put in the cabin and sharpen the axes or shovels instead of trying to keep up with the outdoor chores. And there's always the food in the cabinet to sort through.

On the floor, my father arranges pieces of bark with his foot as if he's playing a game, creating a whole world that is more real to him than the one he is in. I have no idea whether he is acting this way because he's unhappy with the way I'm living my life or because he's unhappy with the way he's lived his. I have no idea whether he feels the shift in our relationship or whether all of his sadness is the sign of something larger. As I look over at him, I realize I don't know what it feels like to be older and feebler than you'd like to be. What I do know is that I miss him—his way of knowing and seeing the world, his way of making me feel safe, like when I was a kid. And I know I'm aware of the arc of a life that is his.

But I don't mention any of what I'm struggling with. Instead, I open the faded ranger book, sit down at the table, and begin catching up on the daily entries I'm required to log as one of my duties.

Later when the rain lets up a little, my father goes out on the stoop carrying his aluminum fly box, and I wonder about the two trout in the bucket in the corner—a scene I'd come to think of as "Still Life with Fish." I wonder about all the sun they're not getting in this cave-like cabin, and about all the air filled with smoke and carbon dioxide from the old woodburning stove. Finally, I have the nerve to walk over to the corner and look down into the metal cook pot. At first, I can only see blackness and shadows, swirling like a kaleidoscope, and then I begin to make out the two trout suspended in water. When I see them and understand what they are, I know, in a moment, that they are dying. Their backs have the white film of death on them. And they are tilting sideways, their bodies caving in to the pull they are feeling.

Someone Else Dies

‹‹‹» ✦ «‹‹›

AN OLD RANGER—he's dead now—once told me that the dispatch office is the heart of any national park. He was right: information constantly flows into the office in one form and pumps out of the office in another. From Memorial Day to Labor Day, in fact, the pulse of Rocky Mountain National Park runs unhealthily high. It's not until late fall, after most dispatchers have returned to their urban lives, that systems in the park start slowing down. During those cold months of the year, a lone ranger riding road patrol might advise that Deer Ridge Junction is socked in or that a dozen elk are grazing through the snow in Upper Beaver Meadows. Otherwise, the park is dead, except for occasional flutters of off-season activity.

These flutters sometimes surprise even the most calm and unflappable dispatchers. The first November I work dispatch, I don't expect the phone call I get one Wednesday from the Boulder Police Department to lead to anything beyond a routine check for a missing person. The passenger vehicle she's after—Colorado Lima-Bravo-5233—doesn't have to belong to someone who has gotten into mischief. Of course, it could, but my job at the moment is only to find out whether the 1979 gold Datsun is at the Longs Peak Trailhead where the Boulder police have reason to believe it might be. If it were summer, I'd phone the ranger station and one or more of the four or five rangers on duty would check through the dozens of cars in the parking lot as if they were doing inventory. But it's not summer. In fact, the road might not even be plowed all the way to the parking lot, and out the high strip of window in the dispatch office, I can see only pregnant snow-sky.

In winter, most park rangers hibernate like marmots, but the ones still stirring sometimes sniff out calls that end up going big. I've worked long enough in Rocky Mountain to know Charlie is like that. When he volunteers to drive up to the Longs Peak Trailhead and reports finding the missing and empty Datsun, I'm not surprised. Once I tell the police dispatcher in Boulder we have the vehicle, she shoots me the facts: the twenty-four-year-old owner of the Datsun has been despondent for weeks, thinks he didn't get into medical school, lost his girlfriend—the stuff of a predictable and touching movie. This information comes to me privately, person to person, dispatcher to dispatcher, but when I swivel my chair away from the telephone and talk into the microphone to tell Charlie, the voice of the dispatch office blabs loud enough for everyone on the NPS frequency to hear. I picture all those sluggish rangers, whether on duty or not, lifting their heads to gaze up towards the flat summit of Longs.

From what Charlie doesn't report, I decide that no obvious clues exist in or around the vehicle. Nosy questions are never proper protocol for dispatchers, and though I'm curious about everything—Is the car cold? Is its hood warm? Are its doors locked? Are its tires chained? Are human footprints visible anywhere and, if so, which way do they go?—I refrain from asking Charlie a thing. Most hikers tend to stick to the widest trail and head for the tallest mountain—at least during the summer months when everyone wants to summit a fourteen-thousand-foot peak. Hiking the 7.5 miles up Longs in winter, however, isn't the same. In winter, there are no wild columbines down by the trailhead. No armies of hikers starting up the trail before dawn. No rock climbers aiming for perfect granite with their magical gear. What it must be up there now is a desert of white cold.

Usually in winter, a park dispatcher works alone, putting entries into the log and waiting for an event to unfold. Sometimes during a search or rescue, the chief ranger or visitor protection specialist appears and disappears and reappears in the doorway, checking on the progress of a search.

When Charlie, aka 212, radios down that he's above Goblins Forest, I type in the exact time (1538) and the exact details (212 advises he is above Goblins Forest). When he asks me to contact Van Slyke to check on his availability, I do the same (212 requests dispatch to contact Van Slyke). Writing the dispatch log is a lot like writing a novel, only I don't have to think. I just sit waiting for the plot and its details to emerge.

If this guy is dead, though, his story will be more than entries in a dispatch log. It will be an official government document stored in an official government file that can become a couple inches thick: a collage of ranger reports, witness reports, graphs, charts, maps, and forms. Most park dispatchers page through these documents during their graveyard shifts as if they're reading ghost stories. Some files even include photographs of the bodies. The truth is, if you want your death documented in detail, it's best to die in a national park. Rangers relish the paperwork and post-incident reviews involved with fatalities when they consider all the work needed to document illegal camping or dogs off leash a mere annoyance. What interests me most is what all this posthumous documentation means and why most park rangers consider the best deaths the ones in the thickest files. As if they're the most significant.

But even thin files make for good drama: a six-year-old male slips on a wet rock beside the Big Thompson River—he is sucked downstream like a twig; a seventeen-year-old male is struck by lightning as he and his girlfriend cuddle under a rock to avoid the rain—she isn't touched; a twenty-one-year-old male falls in a way that all of us joke about—while above Ypsilon Lake taking photographs, he backs into nothing, dropping two thousand feet; a twenty-nine-year-old female lost in a blizzard becomes hypothermic—she experiences sensations of warmth, scattering her mittens, parka, and wool sweater along Thunder Pass; a seventy-three-year-old male suffers a heart attack while driving (probably due to the altitude and his obesity)—he steers his Chevrolet Caprice off Trail Ridge Road and flies, for a moment, his wife copiloting beside him. Of course, not all park deaths are accidental. More than one person has driven up to Rainbow Curve or Rock Cut, where the view dazzles, and taken his or her life.

Park service deaths are the ones I know best. At twenty-four, I've had only a few experiences with anyone I know dying. My father's father, who I barely knew, died of stomach cancer when I was eight years old, and a high school classmate died in a car accident New Year's Eve of my senior year. Until working for the park, though, I never realized unusual deaths could be so common. And I never searched death out, the way I did when dispatched to help look for a twelve-year-old boy who disappeared into the thin mountain air. By the time I was called out, he'd already been missing for three days, and the chances that he'd still be alive, wherever he was, were below zero. There'd been cold weather and sleet. He was lightly dressed when last seen. For eight days, searchers went out, sometimes with dogs. A fortune teller was hired to locate him. She did her work in a Winnebago belonging to the kid's parents and decided—though I don't know how—that he'd hiked over Flattop Mountain to start a new life. There'd been a half moon. There'd been family problems. Finally, the chief ranger called off the search.

A week later, three hikers spotted a blood-stained visor wedged between two boulders and reported its location to park headquarters. It, of course, turned out to belong to the twelve-year-old boy, whose body was found two hours later by a ranger who estimated the fall lines from the location of the visor. According to the official investigation report, the boy most probably slid down a steep snowfield, crashing into the boulders below. These mountains kill. Their rivers pull you in and gobble you up.

Some dispatchers take these kinds of stories to parties, especially Kerry Wright who was always fascinated by the 1970s college boy who must have invited his date for a weekend at Longs Peak Lodge. The couple started up on cross-country skis and were nabbed east of Chasm Lake by a whiteout. From there it's mostly speculation. The college boy did break his leg (and eventually freeze despite packing in a down sleeping bag) and his date apparently started out for help, almost making it. Her body was found beside a boulder and an unlit teepee of twigs. The part of the story Kerry liked most was what she always saved for the punch line: there's no such thing as Longs Peak Lodge. It was just a glossy figment of one poor girl's imagination: a romantic spot with a fireplace and rustic wood interior, mountain meals served next to scenic windows, a dance band playing after 8:00 p.m. The way I figure it, the college boy was grossly uninformed or intentionally gave his date some line. Why else the meager contents of her daypack: a dress, a night gown, and pink hair rollers?

The only structure on Longs Peak is a rustic shelter at 13,400 feet named after Agnes Vaille, the first woman to summit the peak's east face in winter before dying of hypothermia while descending what she'd just conquered. About the size of a walk-in closet, the shelter has thick rock walls, two thin windows, one doorway with no door, and a pointed roof. Just some place to save your life during a storm.

When Charlie is above the shelter, he calls in a 10-55F (park service lingo for fatal accident). With his binoculars, he had spotted a motionless figure slouched on a ledge and he's finally hiked up to its location. I dispatch a helicopter from Denver and advise Charlie on its ETA.

Before my shift ends, the body is brought around to headquarters from the helipad, and Jim Wilson, the east district ranger, asks me to come down to the parking lot as a witness. There's even a form Jim hands me to sign—a ROMO 89 in triplicate—that verifies the possessions belonging to the owner of the gold Datsun, including a quart water bottle with a thick plastic lid, just like the one I carry.

His bottle is half-filled with antifreeze; Jim thinks he died by drinking the other half. I'm not very interested in this young man's possessions, but I nod as Jim calls out each one.

I'm more interested in the body in the back of Jim's Ramcharger—two arms and two legs in the air, his joints bent like a tortured GI Joe doll. He looks so uncomfortable like that—so bulky—so impossible to put in a body bag. It's then that I feel everything inside of me seize up. This is the first body I've been near that hasn't been covered or enclosed. It's the first body I've seen. Frozen. Not just the limbs but the pale hair and lips. The eyes that are both open. His waxy-looking cheeks, cold and stiff to the touch.

There's an Old Dump
Below Lawn Lake

WHEN I WORKED for Rocky Mountain National Park and was stationed in the backcountry at Lawn Lake, I used to walk downhill from the patrol cabin in the evenings and sit on an old rotting log at the dump. It wasn't a working dump filled with milk cartons and orange peels and rich smells, but an eighty-year-old dump, about ten feet square, that Charlie, my supervisor, had shown me the day we packed in supplies. I always felt more comfortable hidden there in the woods than in the patrol cabin which, as the sun went down and before I lit the lanterns, took on the bare, cold feel of a dead cave. At the dump, I'd cradle a cup of coffee in my lap and relax with the objects in front of me: the cans, a wagon wheel, a scoop with a long handle called a fresno. All of them were covered with the same orange-colored crust, as if a heavy syrup had been poured over them and then petrified to a dull glaze. They were themselves, yet not quite themselves. They were in the process of becoming *un-cans* or an *un-wheel* or an *un-fresno*. I was always tired after a full day of patrol, but content, and the dump entertained me, as if I were sitting and admiring a free exhibit in the backcountry. I never stayed after it got dark. I'd return to the cabin until the next evening when I would be lonely and gripped by the impulse for companionship. Then I'd go down to the dump again.

At sunset, all that nature around Lawn Lake wanted my attention—three granite peaks sparkling with alpine glow, solitary spruce trees blackening to triangles, Roaring River pouring greyer and greyer out of the lake as the sky grew darker. The lakeshore itself was studded with rocks; I could stand on one and get a better view of the pink and purple reflections of sky in the water. But there was not, in all of these spectacles, any indication of the relationship between the human and the natural world. Even after working in these scenes of grandeur for days, I still couldn't really understand the mountains and lakes and rivers. But at the dump, I came face to face with historical evidence: the human leavings that were needed to build the Lawn Lake Dam. The fresno, Charlie had told me, was used for digging; the wheel was, no doubt, from the only spring wagon ever to make it up the drainage; and the cans—it took a lot of food to feed all the men who would have been needed to build the dam. I wonder now if this is what I found comforting about the dump: nature had been changed by humans and these were the remainders, the reminders that no one, in 1902 or again in 1911 when the dam was enlarged by thirty-one acres, had bothered to pack out. So, they became part of the landscape—a strange sculpture. A beautiful dump deep in the heart of the woods. An oxymoron.

During one of my visits to the dump, I realized that if looked at on a small enough scale, I could read nature, so it became less overwhelming. An old log, like the one I always sat on to relax, became soil so slowly that I couldn't really miss the process with my exhausted evening eyes, although, at the same time, I couldn't quite see it happening. When I was a camp counselor, my urban campers found this a hard miracle to believe in. It's all cyclical, I'd say, and then I'd simplify, trees turn to logs which turn to soil which turn to trees which turn to logs which turn back to soil. The campers looked doubtful—mouths open, peeking dreamily into their brown lunch bags. That summer I was repeating something I had learned in counselor's training, but the first time I really saw it at the dump, this cycle, no matter how much it seemed a cliché, stunned me into stillness and concentration. One of the logs in the clearing was rotted at both ends, damper and mushier towards the middle, disintegrating until the wood was not in flakes or chips, but had, at some point which I couldn't exactly identify, turned to soil. I scooped up a handful of it, and in my other hand, I scooped up the *real* earth. There was, as far as I could see, no difference between the two. Add to that the little seedling growing out of the log-turned-to-soil and there was, as it were, such a thing as resurrection.

∞

I was at my residence in the front country on a July morning when the Lawn Lake Dam broke like a corral gate being slammed open. Dan Davis, the road patrol ranger on duty, reported the breakage on the NPS frequency, and I remember his usual calm voice sounding as if he couldn't believe his own transmission. He had heard a roar and seen the water flash down the canyon and into Horseshoe Park over five miles from the lake, but there was no rain, no storm, no hint of foreboding before the break happened. This kind of surprise flood was nothing anyone had prepared us for in training, and it was nothing like the Big Thompson flood that happened my first year in the park when 145 people were killed the night I sat working the graveyard shift at the Fall River Entrance as a solid pane of rain distorted the vision of my parked car and the naked flagpole beside it. In the end, the Lawn Lake flood was one big tragedy. Three young campers were killed, one sleeping in his tent at my favorite backcountry campsite. Thirty-one million dollars of damage was caused in a few minutes. One thick scar left zigzagging all the way up the drainage. For days, I couldn't believe that the break had happened.

It wasn't until the last days of August that I was dispatched to the lake, and it was easy to see why the park superintendent had closed the entire area to the public. On the hike up, I climbed over boulders and downed trees and walls of brush, and the trip took a couple hours longer than it usually did. In many spots the trail had been ripped away. In other spots, Roaring River had cut a new bed for itself. I couldn't get to most of the backcountry campsites I always checked whenever hiking past on patrol.

When I arrived at the lake, there was no destruction, but without the dam existing to plug up the south inlet, the landscape had changed, and I stood looking out at a view I no longer recognized. Once holding forty-eight surface acres of water before the dam broke, Lawn Lake now held sixteen, leaving its rocky shoreline exposed like a grey frame encircling the water. The lake itself looked timid, as if it were embarrassed to be what it was before the earthen dam was constructed. That evening when I walked through the woods to the dump, it was eerie—there was no longer a dam, but I was staring at the familiar remains of what had been used to build it.

During three seasons of evenings at the dump, I seemed to have taken for granted that there were two separate cycles discretely in motion as I sat in the twilight: the cycle of human leavings and the cycle of natural change, each decaying in its own slow fashion. This was an assumption that I'd carried around with me like my dark-green daypack. But when I leaned over to touch a can, the calm I usually felt at the dump vanished. The edge of the can crumbled, and the residue remaining in my hand was no different than soil in its color and consistency. The can was no longer the human creation it had been.

That's when I understood I had been playing a trick on myself, separating humans and what we build from the towering trees and the nutrients that feed them. That's when I conflated humans and nature in a way I never had, reformatting the way I saw myself in the world.

∞

A couple years later, after I no longer worked for the park, I first read an essay by Joan Didion in which she imagines the Hoover Dam continuing to stand, presumably forever, after all human life has been wiped out. After first seeing this famous dam, Didion isn't able to shake it, often visiting and once hiring her own personal tour guide, who takes her to places inside the structure that most tourists never see.

I still haven't seen the Hoover Dam (or Boulder City, Nevada, a dump-town that was the by-product of the dam's construction). What I have instead of experience is a three-by-five-inch postcard of the dam that I keep in a file folder and take out every few years. From its aerial perspective, the dam almost sparkles amidst the brown and blue of the mountains and water. Named after Herbert Hoover, who lobbied heavily for its construction during the Great Depression, the dam impounds the Colorado River. I found the postcard at the Herbert Hoover Presidential Library when I lived in eastern Iowa.

What my postcard doesn't emphasize is the massiveness of the dam. One thousand two hundred forty-four feet across, the dam is as thick at its base as a fourteen-lane freeway. Until September 11, when terrorist threats resulted in the construction of a bypass, US Route 93 snaked along the dam's forty-five-foot-wide rim. And the dam is tall. If I stood at its base, and looked up to the sky, I wouldn't see a bird or a plane until I'd looked beyond seven hundred feet of concrete.

Often when I read "At the Dam," I'm seduced into believing—as Didion herself seems to—that the dam is a permanent structure, somehow separate from humans. Able to hold back ten trillion gallons of water in a single day, the Hoover Dam seems like a strange visitor from another planet. A super hero corralling the Colorado River. If it ever broke, there would be ark-worthy flooding all the way to California, but Didion doesn't think it will. "That was the image I had seen always," Didion writes in the final sentence of her essay, "seen it without quite realizing what I saw, a dynamo finally free of man, splendid at last in its absolute isolation, transmitting power and releasing water to a world where no one is."

The last time I finished reading "At the Dam," I had a strong urge to hike the 5.2 miles up to the Lawn Lake Patrol Cabin. I was living in North Carolina at the time with two young daughters, so even getting to the trailhead and assembling my gear would have involved skill and luck far out of my reach, but I fantasized about arriving at dusk, dropping my pack on the cabin's cement stoop, and strolling fifty feet downhill to visit my old friend. As I walked, I'd recognize the feel of the Colorado terrain under my boots and the darkening grey-green color of the Engelmann spruce all around me, and I know I'd be exhausted from the hike, my back a sheet of cold sweat. Only after relaxing against a log or tree with my legs stretched out long and crossed at the ankles would I have enough energy to focus on the angles and shapes and curves that make up the dump. Though in the evening dusk their weird beauty might look familiar and unchanged to me, I'd know that at some point soon enough, and in the most casual of ways, all of this would be gone.

Backcountry Trash (and Other Important Considerations)

1. From Dunraven Glade Trailhead to the North Fork Patrol Cabin

WHEN CHARLIE, my supervisor, drops me off at the trailhead, we both understand that *backcountry patrol* is a euphemism for many duties, including picking up trash. When I post a sign, fell a tree, oil a chainsaw or dig a short-drop privy, there's room for improvement, but when it comes to picking up trash, I'm an expert, spotting every blemish on the trail and then evacuating it. It's like modern dance, lunging down to scoop up a Kleenex or candy wrapper, slipping it in the pocket of my green park service jeans, and continuing on without slowing a step.

Of course, litter in this remote subdistrict of Rocky Mountain National Park is not common, but at any beautiful lunch spot—Dunraven Meadows, Deserted Village—items once packed in a backpack transform into trash: toothpicks, sardine cans, toilet paper in Ziploc bags, the head of a small axe. And there's always the possibility of abandoned apple cores or eggshells or the peels from a banana or orange. Biodegradable trash: the kind even some of my fellow rangers shrug at. "Let a chipmunk enjoy," they say when I point out nonindigenous intruders like pistachio shells spoiling a rock. "What's the big deal?"

Trash rarely appears by accident. Travel experts advise us to pack light, so we throw cigarette butts down when we hike and jettison aluminum cans from our interstate-traveling cars. Historical precedent exists for this behavior: just as our forefathers and mothers abandoned quilts and trunks and rocking chairs from their prairie schooners so they could continue moving westward, we feel compelled to leave our burdensome possessions along the way. The last time I was in the lost-and-found vault at park headquarters amidst the tents and pillows and flashlights retrieved from the backcountry, I realized how heavily some park visitors might feel the weight of history, of knowing what to leave behind.

Some trash even resonates with the historic. I've found thick glass bottles I don't recognize. Rust-covered cans from decades before I was born. Nails and bolts and wire no longer doing their job. Historic trash is my favorite. Little footprints telling me others have been here and seen what I've seen. I know stories about these early litterers: Alexander MacGregor, Frank McGraw, and Windham Thomas Wyndham-Quin (the fourth Earl of Dunraven), who buried a case of whiskey in these mountains that has yet to be recovered. Trash? The mother lode?

And then there's anti-trash: instead of bringing scraps of plastic or nylon or metal into the backcountry, visitors pack bits of nature out. Souvenirs of granite or quartz, cones from an Engelmann spruce, columbines or harebells pressed into two dimensions. All packaged within zippered backpack compartments and taken away to a new home in a drawer or on a mantel. As if the backcountry is one big shop to choose from without paying. I've never caught a camper trying to dig up a square of tundra like car-driving visitors do along Trail Ridge Road, but I have stopped more than one palming a rack from a deer or an elk. *Drop it or you'll pay,* I want to say in a firm voice. Instead I tell them that the park is a museum. The only item legal to remove from its boundaries is trout—but only if you have a license and follow the catch-limit laws.

I collect all imported trash in a huge, clear, double-strength plastic bag that I think of as part of my park service uniform. At the end of a five-day patrol, I lash the bag to the outside of my backpack or throw it over my shoulder and transport it down from the patrol cabin to the trailhead. A grey and green Santa Claus carrying contagions. An exhausted ranger.

2. From the North Fork Patrol Cabin to Lost Lake

On the way up the drainage, I always de-trash the lower campsites, retrieving the shovel I leave stashed in the woods and arriving at a site I know will be vacant because backpackers, like most travelers, have this compulsion to be moving by noon. Behind them they leave static campsite décor that most of them will never see again. A sunken fire grate, silver arrowhead marker, wooden toilet sign bolted to a tree in two places—things not easily stolen.

When I arrive at any one of the sites, I put my shovel down beside the fire grate. From there I radiate out in a bigger and bigger spiral, negotiating trees, bushes, logs, rocks, sweeping the area for more trash—for what has collected since my last patrol and is in plain sight. A kind of general maintenance and tidying up, like dusting. Around the tent pad little pieces of fabric scar the earth. Maybe string. Plastic tent stakes. Safety pins matted down into hard dirt. A half-melted water bottle. A nail piercing the base of a pine. No one would intentionally leave a springy bungee cord or a solitary tent stake behind, but they do. These are reincarnated as trash. And they must, without question, be removed or they will take over. Littering is contagious: a gum wrapper left on a tent pad by one camper brings more wrappers by others who follow.

But the worst kind of trash is not imported—it's indigenous, like ashes and charcoal from fires or pine boughs cut down for a bed. Initials carved on trees are trash too. Rocks blackened in illegal fire rings. Trampled down earth. Whittled sharp sticks. Stripped clean leaves. Trash in the backcountry is anything that wouldn't be where or how it is without the interference of people. I break up fire rings and turn over black rocks. Drag logs to keep tents off fragile clearings. Hide pine boughs in the bushes and wish for Band-Aids to apply to trees' wounds.

Finding a site's fire grate trashed means finding absolutely anything. That's why I wear gloves when groping in a pit searching for what I can't see. I know what people eat by their trash. I know how they live, who they are, what they do. If they love. If I fish out half-disintegrated, freeze-dried food bags, I know the wealthy or inexperienced have been here. If I hook a plastic container made to hold spices or nuts or eggs, I know the kind of camper who pours over acronym-titled catalogues—REI, EMS, MEC—stayed for the night. These campers do not like keeping warm and safe with as little as possible. They are not minimalists. If the ashes are still warm, they are not far off. If the grate is still clean when I arrive, no one has had a fire since my last visit. This usually means no one has occupied the site because few campers anywhere camp without building a fire, whether it's legal to have one or not. A clean fire grate means finding a slip of paper, held in place with a small rock, broadcasting truth from the dark empty pit: ALUMINUM FOIL DOES NOT BURN—PLEASE PACK OUT ALL TRASH. My message to humanity.

There's more than one way to remove ashes from a backcountry fire grate, and the choice you make is an ethical one. Some rangers find a large rock or a stump on the outskirts of the campsite and shovel the ashes behind it. Out of sight, out of mind, until by the end of the summer, campers are virtually surrounded by mounds of ash. A second option involves shoveling ashes into a second huge, clear, double-strength plastic bag and walking them to the river. I make two or three trips: shoveling the ashes in, holding the bag from the bottom away from my uniform, and walking them through the underbrush. At the river, I step carefully onto the rocks and into the roar of the water. Here I let the ashes go: the smoky-white dust of the debris settling on the water's surface, the wind blowing away everything it can, and the pieces of charcoal floating in front of me for an instant before washing down river as they exit the backcountry.

3. From Lost Lake to Mummy Pass

When I patrol above Lost Lake, the world appears trash free. But here's the rub: although fewer backpackers push this close to the clouds, at this elevation everything they do matters. It's no rural legend that alpine flora grows in slow motion. Dwarf willows a few inches tall may be over a hundred years old. Lichens scraped away by a boot take three decades to grow back. The tundra is old fashioned and naked. Wiser than any rain forest. More delicate than fine china.

Up here all evidence of the park service has vaporized. No trails, bridges, boundary markers, earthen dams, log checks, or privies. No wooden signs carved with precise mileage. No switchbacks sculpted in riprap. No backcountry cabin with its horse corral and dark-brown logs fitted perfectly at the joints.

Instead, way above tree line, the mountains line up like soldiers, and I feel as if I'm visiting dear friends. Behind them the Never Summer Range glistens. The sky looks pure, and I should be at the top of my world absorbing the view.

But I know too much. I know some enemies can't be seen—that invisible trash from Denver rains down on this backcountry whenever it wants, littering sulfur dioxide and nitrogen oxide faster than hikers leave cigarette lighters or canisters of white gas. I know pistachio shells and Hershey wrappers, though horrible, are not toxic like the faraway burning of oil and coal. The leaching of nutrients from soil. Because of what I can't see, I have stopped kneeling for handfuls of untreated alpine water when I'm thirsty. Started mourning absent flowers and insects and trout, the boreal toad crouching on the shores of Lost Lake. Invisible trash moves through thin mountain soil like ghosts through doors. Some people don't believe it. Others don't care.

Whenever I'm here looking out on the North Fork subdistrict, I fall from my park ranger pedestal. Not only because I feel the full impact and implication of failure, but also because I don't know what to do. Maybe log the changes. If I could, I'd sniff out the unseen. Vacuum it before it seeps downslope and spreads. Before it taints tarns and snowfields. Before it kills off the snow buttercups and dwarf clover, making way for hardier grasses and sedge. If I could, I'd pack in a giant magnet able to attract acidic pollutants. I'd build a sparkling dome to arch over the tundra like a new sky. Fill my double-strength plastic bag until it's taut.

But invisible trash is abstract and ethereal, ubiquitous and insidious. Impossible to retrieve. Something scientists study year after year. Policy makers work to reduce. Up here above tree line, all I can do is patrol. Feel the full sun on my cheeks. Admire the artwork all around me, the proud postures of Mummy Mountain and Fairchild and Hague. The carpet of tundra falling away toward the north fork of the Big Thompson. That fast, icy river stretching straight through the pines like a silver chain. Lawn Lake at its west end, a glittering pendant nestled in green.

4. *From Mummy Pass Back to the Trailhead*

When I start back down, I don't think about trash or how powerless I am to stop it. Instead I follow the cairns to the trail and take the trail around the lake, over the runoff, through the meadow, down the switchbacks, and past the campsites. It takes over two hours to get to the patrol cabin, and then it's time for dinner and chores and sleep.

In three days, I'll be down at the trailhead, and the drug that is nature will be gone. Charlie will be waiting for me in the light-green, park service Ramcharger, and I'll heft my double-strength plastic bag into the dumpster and get in beside him. We'll drive along the dirt road, Charlie's rock music on the radio, Charlie talking and joking, and we'll both feel the shift of the tires as they move from graveled earth onto smooth pavement. Then we'll start snaking toward town—the one loved by tourists—that radiates more color and shine than I've seen for the past five days. When we reach the highest point of the highway, the valley will open wide like a book. In the distance, we'll see rows of shops selling T-shirts and taffy, and houses will be scattered on the hillside like confetti. We won't talk about any of the trash we can't see. We never mention the tramway on Prospect Mountain, how it reminds me of a thermometer, its red cabin moving straight up the incline in a steady, thick line.

Over Mummy Pass

IT'S LATE AFTERNOON. The whole day: rain, slow drizzling rain, and tense skies. At a faster-than-comfortable pace, I hike toward Mummy Pass with a full pack over my rain jacket. I need to get up and out of this drainage and down to the North Fork Patrol Cabin by dark. The tundra is slippery, the switchbacks muddy. Little flowers—the maroon and purple pincushions—grow close to the ground the only way they can and seem to be drowning. The marmots this far in the backcountry are wild and shy, suspicious of hikers. I keep looking for them at each outcrop, expecting to be startled by their sharp whistles and knowing they can trick you into thinking they're rocks by not moving. My legs surprise me with their stiffness. I know I have started out too late.

Sometimes I crave a different, less adventurous disposition instead of always biting off so much that I almost choke. I could be back at the Lawn Lake Patrol Cabin, where I have been stationed the past four days, lighting the kindling in the woodburning stove or getting the bedding out of the bedding box. I could be going for water with the ten-gallon plastic container knowing that bringing it back will be difficult because it's uphill and water can be heavy. When I'm stationed at Lawn Lake, I patrol the campsites around the lake three, four, sometimes five times a day. Rituals become paramount: drinking instant coffee mixed with instant chocolate and instant milk; hanging up the long-sleeve, grey uniform shirt on the one hanger at the end of the day; watching the sun tuck itself in for the night. Here on this traverse, the little patrol cabin is completely hidden, and there is no cement stoop to sit on at sunset, no cup of mountain brew steaming for me anywhere in the rain.

Before topping the pass, I experience one of those acts of nature I thought I understood. Lightning, and it's quick: a wide line of neon fire so close I can't see it. I'm standing and then—simply—I'm down. Stunned. Feeling electricity crackle alive in the air and hearing echoes of a noise so loud it hurts my ears. There's no smell of burning, no smoke, no damage, and when I look for it, the lightning has vanished, leaving the ordinary sky above the pass and the top of Mummy Mountain, as rock-like as ever, rising above it.

Pulling back my hood, I feel the rain wet my forehead and run in little fingers through my scalp. Lightning, I know, can target the same place twice. Most moves from cloud to cloud. Often, it's forked. The air above me seems taut, like it was the day Pat motioned me down from the summit of Longs, dropping her ice axe and yelling at me to get back. Her eyes bright fire. Her black hair standing out from her head with more electricity than anyone could ever get from brushing. She knew that electric fields stretch through space, that more than one person has been hit by lightning in this national park and that many die, although a direct strike doesn't have to kill you. One boy a few years back was fine afterward: a black burn spot on the sole of each foot.

But I haven't been hit, or I don't think that I have. What was hit was bare tundra, fifty feet ahead on the pass, and although I know electric current can surge through the earth with as much force as it speeds through sky, I know I have been spared.

Still, something has happened. I have been on this pass many times before but never lying spread-eagle in the rain with so much quiet. Never inhaling the rain as it comes down, my mouth open and kissing the sky. Never feeling what seems like joy rise in my chest like warmth. Sitting, I unzip a side pocket of my pack, get out my water bottle, and take a long drink. The whole world has never tasted so good.

Rising, I steady myself. The leather of my boots has finally given way to water, and I am drenched everywhere, but not cold. It's 4:45: five miles to go. I'm surprised my watch still works. I adjust my pack with what feels like affection, buckle the waist strap, cinch up the smaller straps at my shoulders, feel for the radio at my hip. More rituals, similar to the ones I did before leaving the patrol cabin: bolt the windows, replenish the wood, sweep the floor, fill the fuel tanks, secure the bedding box, lock the door like anyone would lock up a home. As I descend into the North Fork drainage, I can almost feel those three, old, uncaring mountains—Mummy and Hague and Fairchild—watching me from behind.

When I Leave

◄═ ✦ ═►

NO MATTER which way I start up to the North Fork Patrol Cabin from town, it's hard work. If I take the old horse trail from the McGraw Ranch, the route flies straight up the ridge and then down switchbacks so steep that my knees buckle and the next day even my shins ache. If I take the Forest Service trail in, I end up winding through scrubland—as if I'm lost or have no place to be. Coming in fifteen miles from Lawn Lake or twenty from Red Feathers is not practical in one day. And having someone drive me through the Cheley Boys' Camp in the Ramcharger is like running an obstacle course—there are four gates to unlock and then lock back up, one knee-deep river to cross (in four-wheel drive), and wild archery arrows to dodge. This approach does end up being the fastest, but it's not easy hiking. And no matter which way I go, I feel the pull of the front country for well over an hour before surrendering to the backcountry terrain. It's always hard to get back home.

But when I do arrive in the clearing and see the cabin with its naked flag pole in front of it, I feel as if I'm hooked back into a web where everything fits. I rest by the river, enjoying the last of the sun and feeling my sweat dry. I don't know whether it's taking my pack off or breathing the thinner air or something else, but I'm always so light when I first arrive in the North Fork. And usually this lightness stays with me until later, until after I've begun the inside chores like priming the stove and lighting the kindling. Then I begin to feel grounded. Then I begin to feel the rhythm of the place and the cabin settle around me like skin.

Whenever I first unlock the door—whether I've been gone for a few weeks or a few days or the whole winter—I have this feeling that everything inside has been holding its breath waiting for my return. Silence that has been bolted up is so quiet. But, of course, the stasis I imagine everything has been in while I was away is an illusion; between my stays someone else is almost always stationed here. It's just that all of us leave everything exactly where it should be, and if a thing is out of place it's as obvious as night since everything in this cabin comes in pairs: two lanterns, two dish pans, two mattresses, two beds (bunk), two fire packs, two piss pumps, two tables, two axes. It's a practical male house. We're always prepared for a split axe handle or the cracked globe of a Coleman lantern.

What I can't understand is how everything in the cabin feels as if it belongs to me. I always hike in wearing a full pack filled with fresh food and the clean socks and T-shirts I spread out on the bottom bunk. Everything else is the property of the US Government, except someone's copy of *The Shining* on the shelf and the cracked mirror Bob and Randy and Charlie use for shaving. What I'd like to think is that there is some easy equation for figuring out where we belong—something like the right place is equal to so many hours a person spends in a location—but the variables never line up. Maybe we don't need to belong to a place that is ours, but just to feel like it is and like it could be if it were. Or maybe the right place is wherever we are and not wishing to be somewhere else. Or where we have everything that we need, so that this is Bob's cabin when he needs it and Randy's or Charlie's when either of them needs it, too. So that when no one needs it, it is no one's. Or it's all of ours at once—and we're an odd family tied to a place we never share at the same time. But I doubt any of my coworkers ever think about this cabin when they're not here, and I can't see myself asking them whether or not they do. Maybe the three of them only think of this space as an office or motel room. Maybe all any of us needs is a place where we can breathe without a tight feeling.

Whenever I'm stationed here, I want curtains for the windows, and sometimes in the evenings they become an obsession. I want them calico like the ones at the Lawn Lake Patrol Cabin, and by the end of my last season, I make them myself on my own time. I don't care whether I'm reimbursed for the fabric by the US Government. I don't care whether anyone knows I am the one who sewed them. They will just appear at both windows on my last day of patrol before hiking out. In blue and yellow and red. Like the magpie who brings back pieces of colored string for the inside of her nest, I will pack my curtains into the North Fork and add them to its interior, knowing that once hung, they will no longer be mine, but by bringing them in I will be leaving my signature on two of the walls. My mark—more civilized than urine. One that will linger for who knows how long after I'm gone.

Going to Die

⚏ ✦ ⚏

"I NEVER have held death in contempt, though in the course of my explorations I have oftentimes felt that to meet one's fate on a noble mountain, or in the heart of a glacier, would be blessed as compared with death from disease, or from some shabby lowland accident. But the best death . . . is hard enough to face, even though we feel gratefully sure that we have already had happiness enough for a dozen lives."

John Muir 1838–1914
Cause of death: pneumonia
Location of death: California Hospital
City: Los Angeles

∞

FATALITIES DURING CLIMBS ON MOUNT RAINIER
(1897–1979)

Data Sources are National Park Service, Mountain Rescue Association,
and the American Alpine Club

YEAR	DATE	NAME(S)	PARTY SIZE	CAUSE
1897	7/27	Prof. Edgar McClure	large	Fall from rock during night
1909	0/14	T. V Callaghan, Joseph W. Stevens	3	Disappeared at summit in storm
1911	8/-	Legh O. Garrett	1	Disappeared in storm near top
1916	9/18	J. A. Fritsch	7	Died three days after surviving fall in crevasse
1921	8/16	Jack Meredith	7	Fall from Little Tahoma
1929	7/2	Forrest G. Greathouse, Edwin A. Wetzel	6	Slide into crevasse at 12,000 feet
1931	7/5	Robert Zinn	2	Slide into crevasse
1936	1/-	Delmar Fadden	1	Fall, then frozen in descent of Emmons Glacier
1941	8/10	Leon Brigham, Jr.	5	Fall into crevasse, Russell Glacier
1957	9/1	William Haupert	12	Crushed during collapse of snow bridge
1957	11/30	Lowell Linn	1	Disappeared in snowstorm
1959	9/2	Calder T. Bressler	large	Pulmonary edema at summit
1967	9/10	Elmer and Davis Post	3	Slide into crevasse, died of exposure
1968	6/15	Dr. James M. Reddick	3	In cave during snowstorm, exposure
1968	6/23	Patrick Chamay	4	Pulmonary edema on upper Liberty Ridge
1968	9/12	Milton J. Armstrong	1	Probably exposure; body later found above Camp Muir
1969	6/15	George T. Dockery	5	Rockfall on Curtis Ridge
1969	7/13	Mark Kupperberg, David Stevens	large	Slide into crevasse on Winthrop Glacier
1971	8/1	Michael Ferry	5	Fall into crevasse on Ingraham Glacier
1974	11/18	David Taylor	2	Snow avalanche on Success Cleaver
1975	8/14	Mark Jackson	3	Rockfall on Mowich Face
1977	2/16	Jack Wilkins	4	Uncontrolled glissade off Success Cleaver
1977	7/6	Dean Klapper	5	Into crevasse during sitting glissade on Emmons Glacier
1977	9/7	Mary Gnehm	11	Slide of roped party on upper Ingraham Glacier
1978	5/01	Todd Davis	3	Avalanche down Fuhrer Finger
1978	9/8	Shirli Voight, Guillermo Mendoza	2	Climb into storm on Ingraham Glacier
1979	3/4	Willi Unsoeld, Janie Diepenbrock	21	Slab avalanche on upper Cowlitz Glacier

∞∞∞

Elevations over ten thousand feet can make the human body give out. Is it the beauty of it all? The close-up, on-high perspective of peaks and canyons and rocks? The sincere illusion that we really can see forever? The intimacy of cloud kissing crag? Is it really surprising that people drive up to alpine overlooks and take their lives?

I'm not saying a healthy body will just give in, but I am saying that a body that's already feeble in some way—overly unhappy, overly exerted, overly old, overly overweight—can be pushed over the edge at this height. All the seasonal employees who work at Rocky Mountain National Park's Alpine Visitor Center, that lonely building at almost twelve thousand feet, are certified emergency medical technicians and the supervisors are usually men or women with thick arms who can continuously pump on someone's chest, like one of those seesaw oil drills you see on the flatlands. The Alpine Visitor Center is the only place for first aid along one of the highest paved highways in the United States. It's a place supposedly open from Memorial Day to Labor Day, though the road usually isn't plowed until mid-June and summer blizzards can always keep visitors from arriving. It's a place with oil-flush toilets because it's tricky to pump water up so high. In the winter, winds are measured at speeds of over 150 miles an hour by instruments known to blow apart by December. The huge logs on the visitor center's roof are not for decoration; they're to hold the roof on. These winds can whip you around the parking lot and lift you flying into the air. Up here it can take one hundred years for a square of tundra to grow back and one hundred dollars in park service fines if you're the one caught digging for a souvenir of sod. The only animals that live year-round at this elevation are ptarmigans and pikas. As far as I can tell, it's too high for most insects. Is it possible we don't belong here? Is it any surprise that a few people every year get out of their plains-mobiles and swoon into cardiac arrest?

∞

Twenty-five years ago, you might have found me on the face of Notchtop poised on a nub of rock with my weight over my hips and my twenty-two-year-old hands, tanned and strong as they'll ever be, not gripping the granite but finessing a balance. I still remember the climb's one difficult move, which I tried a dozen times in my mind before reaching for a hold and stretching away from safety. My stomach went hollow—the same way it still does right before I speak to a room filled with people—and for one moment I forgot that Pat had me on belay. The rope, of course, was my lifeline dangling down from her.

It was one of those beautiful days of life. Perfect blue sky and sparkling granite. Once we'd gotten over the crux, the climb was finished, and we scrambled to the summit. I still remember coiling the rope and looking down on birds flying below us. I still remember the brilliant taste of our canned sardine lunch—and the wonderful freedom of taking off our shirts for the sun. We were two young women in the mountains with no one else around as far as we could see. For those few minutes, I felt as high as I sometimes feel right after sex. I also felt a sensation that seemed very close to death.

◇◇◇

Delmar Fadden before and after his solitary winter ascent of Emmons Glacier in January 1936.

◇◇◇

After I worked in Rocky Mountain National Park, one of my closest friends, who lived in Seattle at the time, gave me a book on climbing Washington's Mount Rainier for my twenty-eighth birthday. I knew even before reading that one of the last chapters, "Mountain Tragedies," would be the best. In the world of mountaineering, *tragedy* is a euphemism for death, and all the little subsections—"A Slip on Hard Ice," "Party Slides into Crevasse," "Death on Liberty Ridge," "Triple Summit Tragedy"—went down like pills when I finally read them. On the one hand, I'm fascinated by people falling and crashing and being buried alive. My pulse rises, and I feel goose bumps on my skin even when the death doesn't involve the cold. I don't think it's because the accounts are so well written. I think it's because the suspense of death is easy to work into words. I used to read "Mountain Tragedies" with the same satisfaction I've seen other people get from watching murder and horror movies on TV, neither of which I'm able to sit all the way through.

On the other hand, these accounts don't have to be read just as tragedy. Heroes as well as victims star in these pages. Ranger Charlie Browne (his real name) was awarded the first citation ever given for heroism by the Department of Interior for his recovery of a quite-dead body from a dangerous crevice. Ranger Bill Butler was recognized for his search and evacuation operations by President Franklin D. Roosevelt, who gave him a permanent position in the park service. Some heroes, however, become victims. In 1959 the pilot of a small plane and his passenger crashed into a snowfield while attempting to fly oxygen cylinders to a suffering hiker. All three died.

∞

A paradoxical juxtaposition from one of Pat's letters:

An Emergency Room doc died while hiking alone in the Cascades in August. He was probably in his late thirties and had a couple of young kids. Apparently, he was hiking alone on a trail that was a little tricky in terms of exposure and route. The weather turned foul, with temperatures dropping 15 degrees and hail. He decided to go for it and must have slipped off a cliff. He broke his neck and died instantly. Freaky. This guy was both young and healthy, doing the things he loved . . .

. . . I haven't been to the woods since our trip into the Wind River Range and miss it already.

∞

Vertical-line deaths, the kind of death where you move from a higher to a lower point, happen often in the mountains. It's the kind of death that follows an abbreviated and simplified version of a section of Newton's *Principia*: whatever goes up has, of course, to come down. You're above a glacier or snowfield and you slip. You're driving a winding mountain road and you fly off. You're at the summit of a peak and, all of a sudden, you're not. Quick as a blink. This is the kind of death that can't happen on the horizontal line of the prairie. And actions that have no repercussions in the flatlands—tripping, say, over the roots of a tree—can cost you your life in the mountains. This happened to one of Pat's friends: a forty-three-year-old mountain runner who caught his Reebok on a rock and fell two thousand feet. It happened to the ex-girlfriend and ex-climbing partner of someone we both knew: after a difficult climb, the twenty-six-year-old ballerina unroped, took off her helmet, lost her balance, and dropped down the wall she had worked so hard to get up.

These are the kinds of deaths that shouldn't be told to parents, grandparents, friends, colleagues, and most acquaintances. An old boyfriend once urged me to ride the bumper cars if I wanted a thrill. My father, without asking permission, cut the climbing rope I was storing in my parents' basement into three pieces and used them to fashion a colorful railing around the backyard deck he was building. Even my husband stops listening when words like *carabiner*, *crampon*, *belay*, *traverse*, and *scree* sneak into my sentences. If you insist on talking about mountain deaths, be prepared for a clamor: What a waste, the person you're talking with will say. How stupid. What's the point?

∞

Whenever I think about Jeff Christensen, a seasonal ranger hiking the North Fork twenty years after I did, I feel as if I'm thinking about myself. The last time I did Jeff's hike, it was my final July in the park. I was on routine patrol with my daypack, the sun hot at such high elevations, my hair braided and hanging like an exclamation point down my back. I was, like Jeff was planning to do, hiking down alone from the summit of Ypsilon after meandering up the backs of Chapin and Chiquita. I was, as he'd planned to do, negotiating a more treacherous loop toward Spectacle Lakes, instead of going back out, Hansel-and-Gretel style, the way most hikers do. The radio on my belt played static, like it often does in the Mummy Range, and the day was mine. I remember feeling moved as I lingered on a ledge admiring the view. Below me, Spectacle Lakes had emerged like the pair of glasses they are named for. Above me, the summit of Ypsilon sparkled like an angry, grey tooth.

When I visualize Jeff, I imagine his blond hair, his careful smile, and his thirty-one-year-old eyes, all of which featured in the national news for several days in July and August of 2005. In the photograph, he's wearing his short-sleeve, park service shirt, and without much effort I can picture him picking his way through some of the more vertical terrain in the North Fork and feel his frustration as he realizes he's started out too late to complete the route that he'd planned. Usually I imagine him with a forest-green daypack, his thumbs looped in the straps at his chest, so his arms rest against his sides chicken-wing style, the way I hike. In my imagination, I see a young ranger hiking fast and doing the kind of patrol that he's supposed to do for his job, and then I see nothing. Maybe a stumble.

What I imagine next is the world a couple hundred feet below where he just was, the silence all around interrupted by the call of a curious falcon startled by a sudden new neighbor tumbling from nowhere and striking his head. Then I see Jeff fumbling for his radio and wrapping his injured skull with a makeshift T-shirt tourniquet before finding enough strength to continue hiking to the spot where his body was discovered nine days later among boulders and brush. Although investigators claim that all rounds of Jeff's ammunition were accounted for, I sometimes still imagine him squeezing the trigger on his park service issue pistol and hear the snap of gunshots ricocheting from empty peak to empty peak as he realizes, even through all of his injuries, that this call for help was his best hope.

According to several newspaper accounts, Jeff once told his parents not to cry for him if he died while at work in the mountains because he would have died doing what he loved. In the first news account I read, these words are paraphrased, as if his parents are casually remembering what Jeff had said. In later accounts, similar words are quoted as if they have become more accurate, as if the parents' memories had zeroed in on the truth that they didn't know would be so relevant when they heard their son say it. Sometimes I wonder about the context of the parents' report and how that private information ever reached the press. Sometimes I imagine their grief and flinch, remembering that after I had children, I gave birth to my own fear of heights. What I have never wondered while sitting at the table in my early-morning North Carolina kitchen is how to interpret or analyze what Jeff said.

II. FAR

On Not Marrying
a Ranger

<small>⋙ ✦ ⋘</small>

WHEN I WAKE in the tent, everything is black. Outside is a silence that means no wind, no rain. Inside I am floating, swaddled in the same blue sleeping bag I used in the backcountry when I was a ranger. Over me, the tent's dome seems smooth and firm but more flexible than the A frame roof of the backpacking tent I used before my marriage. I can hear my daughters breathing beside me. We are triplets, soaking up what we need.

What I should feel is contentment, the magic humans sometimes experience when our minds intersect with our bodies and both are at peace. What I feel instead is the hum of my own radar, the nag we feel when we have lost something that we just had within reach. Even before groping in the tent and sinking my hand into the softness of Kevin's sleeping bag, I suspect that he's gone, and when I slip on my boots and fleece jacket and unzip the two tent doors, my stomach goes hollow.

Above me the stars are scattered over the universe like salt. The moon is a shy one, but I can still see to make out the campsite—the long picnic table with no Kevin priming the stove, the soggy fire pit with no Kevin arranging the kindling, the collapsible camp chair with no Kevin lounging about. Hide-and-seek, I think without humor; I'm not used to my husband disappearing into the night.

Twelve hours earlier when it was our turn to check into Glacier Basin Campground, I pulled up beside the little ranger station booth. It had just started to sprinkle, and the woman working the information window, according to a protocol I remember well, was wearing her heavy beaver skin hat with its brim parallel to the ground and her long-sleeve, grey dress shirt decorated with an official gold name tag and Department of Interior ranger badge. From my position sitting in the car and her position framed above me in the window, I couldn't tell whether she was wearing the dark-green dress skirt or the dark-green dress pants.

"Hi," I said through the mist, and as I looked at her, waiting for whatever came next, I felt nostalgic—not so much for sitting in a little ranger station, which I did my first season at this park, but for the rest of the life I had those seven years. A life where I thought an eight-hour shift wasn't so much the main focus of a day, as a blip in its rhythm.

A life where many of my colleagues and I thought of this landscape not so much as a national treasure, but as a natural playground where we could run and climb and scramble. Our idea of relaxation was hiking up to the boulder field on Longs Peak and watching the moon rise before hiking down seven miles with headlamps. On days off, we were up at 4 a.m. climbing peaks before the afternoon storms moved in. We slept with our radios on and nearby, hoping to be called out on any search or rescue or hot spot that might materialize when we weren't on duty. We dug snow caves. Bouldered. Backpacked. Wore crampons. Walked the Continental Divide. Ran trails that most visitors never hiked. Often these were not planned activities. They were what made up the daily fabric of the life we lived—like brushing our teeth.

This woman at the Glacier Basin Campground, though, did not look as though she had been living my life of long ago. About sixty, maybe retired from another career and working at the campground seasonally, she seemed to be part of the new wave of rangers I'd noticed working in the front country these past few years—as if all the real rangers I aligned myself with were hidden from the public. Should I, I wondered, tell her I once wore the same park service uniform that she was wearing? That I, too, was employed in this very park twenty years ago patrolling the North Fork subdistrict and before that working the dispatch office and before that collecting the park's two-dollar entry fee? Would she care? Would she know what to do with comments like that? Would she nod as if we shared a special history and a park service bond? Or would she smile, merely hand me the campground map and direct me out past the RV sites to the few drenched tent pads at the back of the campground?

"Mom," I heard my oldest daughter whisper as I put the car in gear ready to drive out toward Loop C, "Tell her you used to be a ranger."

In some sense, I have always been park-ranger material. Whenever I want I can picture the first time I went to a national park: my father sitting at the wheel of our station wagon, tanned arm out the window and bent at the elbow like a triangle, looking for a campsite. He looped around and around the campground with tense patience. Finding a space was something of an art for my father, like everything he did, and I was happily right there with him, evaluating the pros and cons of each possibility. At one point, when he wasn't quite sure about a space, he urged my mother and brothers out of the car at a probable site, giving them squatters' rights, as he continued looking with me still in the car, in case he found another better site around the next bend in the next loop. During the first part of the search, though, my mother sat in the passenger's seat, maybe thinking about all the dirt out the window, while my brothers sat in the back seat looking for deer or, maybe, something bigger. When we found the best spot, we set up the heavy green canvas tent under the command of my father and draped the site's picnic table in a red-and-white checked sheet of oil cloth that I learned to love. On one end of the table, my father placed our dark-green, rectangular-shaped Coleman stove. Not far from the table, kissing a tree, our lantern hung from a nail. On the right side of the tent's entrance, next to the canvas walls and elevated off the ground on two parallel logs that my father had laid at the perfect distance, sat our aqua cooler filled with the food we'd bought at the little store in Jackson Hole.

What I remember most about our first site in Yellowstone National Park was my father's frequent order to "go get kindling" and arrange the twigs in piles according to size. For my brothers this usually meant going behind the tent and whipping rocks through the air. For me it meant gathering wood before balancing on a piece of half-submerged granite. I still remember the smell of pine. I still remember the air being almost too dry to breathe. And I still remember the sun warming the top of my head like a hand. One afternoon, from nowhere a fly landed on my bare arm and lifted off and landed again. All I heard was its buzz and then the stop of its buzz, and for a moment that's what mattered.

Eight days ago, when my husband and I bought our brand-new tent, Kevin had turned to me at the REI cash register. "You realize," he'd said, "this thing costs more than a hotel room." His joke wasn't funny to me. I had, in truth, compromised on this purchase, opting for an REI brand-name tent on sale instead of the more streamlined and expensive Patagonia tent that I really wanted. But when I shook the beige and brown REI monstrosity from its carrying duffle in Glacier Basin, I began to like it. It was, for one thing, as light as air—almost like chiffon. Even my daughters could help pitch it, clicking open the thin tent poles and threading them through the sleeves of the tent without me telling them how, as if they'd done this chore before. At one point, even Kevin began threading and we put the poles in the grommets—with me barely looking at the instructions— and our little vacation home morphed into a huge curved shape that was taller than I am.

"Wow," I said, realizing how big my life had become. The girls squealed and moved in their toys and rolled out their sleeping bags, dragging in the wet earth and ignoring what I said about leaving their shoes by the door. They arranged ballerina pillows along one of the thin walls and decided who was sleeping where and in what direction we should put our heads.

"One chore down," Kevin said, humoring me, but I couldn't tell if anything about putting up this tent could really please a boy from Philadelphia. Mostly he seemed interested in preparing dinner, and as I watched him cut carrots, he kept checking the clouds—as if that would prevent more rain from falling.

Now only eight hours later, I am standing alone in the middle of our campsite—a pose that is not new to me. Even at night I have often found myself in places more remote than this soaking in the chill and feeling the beat of the earth. What is new is Kevin's absence. The last time I was certain of where he was, I could pick out his breathing, strong and regular, like a metronome. Before that, we had been taking turns reading the girls a book illustrated with mountain animals.

"Are there bears in these woods?" our youngest daughter had asked as she took her turn holding the flashlight.

"Not really," Kevin had said after a pause, "only rain." His were the last words spoken before the girls drifted off. In the perimeter of the flashlight's orb, I saw them curled around themselves, and I started to drift off too.

Wondering now what to do next, I find Kevin. He's beyond the picnic table reading in our car, sitting in the driver's seat and looking more comfortable than he could ever look in a tent. I see that now. I see that I've married someone for whom camping will never come naturally no matter how hard I wish it would. When trying to refuse my offers of sleeping on the ground, Kevin always argues that being trapped in a tent is like being wrapped in a shroud, but until now I hadn't entirely understood that he was serious, that the flimsy nylon which keeps me feeling close to the natural world keeps him feeling breathless and anxious. Even in our new spacious purchase that was meant to be a solution, he must be reacting to what he calls the very still tent air and its casket-like darkness.

Finally, looking at him sitting there in the middle of the black night, I am okay with offering my daughters this gift of camping myself, this gift which neither one of them might like in the end, this gift that only one parent picked out for them although the other submitted to the routine of outdoor living more than once to please me. I am okay with knowing that camping is my love, one that strengthened me and my idea of who I am and how I move in the world and that not everyone feels content living with trees or, for that matter, dying as part of the natural cycle of life. Sometimes I'm okay with all of that, and I wonder if I make as much noise as I can—stomping my feet and coughing into the cold night—whether Kevin will recognize these sounds as mine and not be startled.

When I walk over to the car, I knock on the driver's side window and my husband gets out of the car and stands beside me. "How is it?" I ask, nodding at the Ann Patchett book in his hands. It's *Truth and Beauty*, the same copy I finished a couple days ago that he'd barely started before we left for this trip. As far as I can tell, he's on the last few pages, his eyes red and tired, as if he's been traveling from a faraway place, as if he really doesn't want to be reading, even a book as good as this one.

"She's about to die," he says finally.

"Did you sleep at all?" I ask, but I don't really expect an answer, and I'm pretty sure that next time I take the girls camping I won't try to persuade him to come along.

In a few hours, it will be morning. Checkout time at Glacier Basin is 11:00 a.m., but we'll be gone before that, shoveling our sleeping bags and tent into the back of the station wagon because everything will be damp. We might even stop at the Donut Haus on our way down to the valley. Our girls would like that. For now, we'll let them sleep. For now, we'll lean against the car and look up at the whole spread of the sky.

"There's Draco," Kevin says, and I know he's right, but at that moment I don't care that he's better at identifying stars through the clouds than I am. I put my head on his shoulder. What I'm feeling instead of irritation is closeness to someone I love, the hugeness of nature pushing down on us, the moon blotted out like a beautiful smudge.

No More to the Lake

⋘ ✦ ⋙

EVERY TIME I read E. B. White's "Once More to the Lake," it sends my head floating, and I feel so close to White's words that they seem suspended inside of me. It's an essay about memory and family and returning to a place that has been part of a person's life since childhood. I love the description of the outboard motors sounding like mosquitoes. I love the togetherness of father and son. I love the storm at the end. And I love the way White negotiates what he calls the grooves of his mind and reflects on the past at the same time that he experiences the present. He published the essay in his early forties, and I know now it takes that much time to appreciate the patterns in our lives.

There's a lake in my life like White's, and over the years I've come to realize that having a lake of your own might be a prerequisite for falling in love with "Once More to the Lake" in the way I have. At least this has been my theory the past couple semesters I've taught the personal essay, since most of the students who read White aren't very enthusiastic about his summer trip and the quiet, everyday, life-and-death events that happen during that week. I sometimes think it's only students like Cory, a young woman who used to vacation at a White-like lake in Maine, who defend White's essay. After reading "Once More to the Lake," Cory went on to write poems about her own lake and the loons that live there and the father who fished by her side.

My lake is in the North Woods of Wisconsin, surrounded by birch trees and decorated with an island, and I arrived there for the first time in the black of night, my father gripping the wheel as he steered a maze of county roads, finally parking in an empty meadow beside Guth's. Guth's Tavern is where all the islanders always parked their cars and where Leonard or Herb Guth, or one of their sons, readied the motorboats that had been waiting the long Wisconsin winter for their noisy lives to begin again. My first time to the lake I was five months old, and my mother remembers that there was no boat waiting for us, so my father walked out onto Guth's pier and untied a boat that wasn't his to row. The moon was barely there, my mother remembers, and she says that she felt like a refugee with a scarf over her head and a bundle that was me in her arms. I like to think that as my father rowed to the island under all those specks of light the sky reached down to kiss me.

If that wasn't when I was injected with the spirit of the place, it might have happened the next day when my father carried me along the one string of trail circling the island and walked into a hornet nest. He was stung three times, and I was stung thirteen, my little body rising like a loaf of bread so that all the elders on the island came around to see whether I should be rushed to the hospital in Rhinelander.

Unlike White's family, my family didn't return to our lake "summer after summer, always on the first of August." In fact, after I was three, we didn't go again until my brothers were born and I was twelve and my father's younger brother held the title to the cottage. There is a big difference between renting a place at a lake, like White did, and staying at a lake because your extended family owns property and a relative sometimes invites you to stay on it for free. Back in 1896, my great-grandfather bought an island membership that allowed him to build a fishing cabin that he passed down to my father's mother and that would one day tell me where I come from in a way that White's rented lodge never could inform him. Over the years, my grandparents added a front porch on to the main structure and then a back porch and then a sleeping porch so that the floors sloped slightly upwards and downwards like waves as you moved from room to room, and we all felt like we were walking on water, not wood. The first evening we arrived, my brothers and I stood around the cottage studying the paneled walls as if we were adults in a museum. There was a photograph of our grandfather we barely knew wearing a white button-down shirt and smiling in a rowboat. There was a shelf of old hardbound books that someone had read. There was a fishing pole mounted horizontally along the wall. There was a big map of the lake with the depths of its waters penned in with blue ink and all its bays spreading out like fat fingers. There was a catalogue of the names and heights of my ancestors, including my father, penciled into the wood as they had grown taller over the years. And there was comic relief: the drawing of a little cartoon character driving his speedboat away without knowing it was tied to the dock behind him. "I'll be back," the caption said.

When we vacationed at the lake those four years of my adolescence, my oldest brother and I ran with the other boys and girls whose parents had grown up with my father. Some days we were on the water swimming and rowing and fishing. Some days we stayed on land and lured crawdads from the rocks with bacon or played hearts around some-one's wood table. The weather controlled our adventures. I water-skied behind a 12-horsepower fishing boat and canoed through reeds to watch raccoons clean their food. I learned the shape and size of a musky and that my grandfather could only land his "big one" by shooting the fish in its head with a pistol. When an islander went to the mainland and brought the mail back over, a couple of us girls would deliver it by dinghy, and I felt transported, as if we were living a scene from another, more enchanted time. One day, my brother and I and two other kids took canoes all the way across Outlet Bay to see whether we could find the little stream that emptied out of the lake. We packed a lunch and glided in pairs across the water to a place we'd never been. The sun was bright, and the lake was flat as if someone had pulled it taut. For most of the day the canoes, one red and one green, traveled side by side, and even though we never found what we were looking for, we found out how much we liked being that far out on the water.

I don't think I realized it then, but during those four years of my adolescence, I was especially attuned to my father's longing for this place I loved. Of course, he summered there as a kid, year after year, but by his early twenties, he seemed to have lost any grip he might have had on the cottage by distancing himself from his parents and spending the rest of his life longing to get it, or something like it, back in his hands. I was never told exactly why my one uncle controlled the cottage and why my father's two older brothers had cottages of their own on different lakes in different states. I was also never warned by any adult that my father's frequent talk about getting a cottage of our own would end up just being words. Probably nobody knew. I realize now that this is what my father did well: he pursued options or, more accurately, this one dream. Looking back, I'm not sure he even enjoyed being on the island those years of my adolescence. He did stoke the wood stove with what looked like love before the rest of us got out of our warm beds. And he did lug rocks from the shallow water over to where he was trying to build a rock jetty. But he didn't fish with us like White fished with his son in "Once More to the Lake," and I didn't have the sense that my father reflected on family and the passing of generations in the thoughtful way that White did. There was something desperate and confusing about my father's relationship to this place that he treasured but didn't possess, almost as if he wanted to infect his children both with an identity connected to place and with an intense obsession for a place we'd probably never get as our own. One year he even sent us all to the lake for a month while he stayed home working in Omaha, and my mom let my oldest brother drive the aluminum fishing boat to the island when we arrived.

When Mr. Fulton, the widower who lived next door, died one winter, my father took that as an opportunity. He called Mr. Fulton's son in California about buying his father's cottage, but instead of letting go of the property, the son began visiting the lake each summer, almost as if my father's call had reminded him about this place that belonged to his family. Another winter a cottage on the mainland burnt down and my father got word that its lot was for sale. From our dock you could see the new clearing made by the fire, and my father eyed that space from a distance for a couple days before going across the lake to take a look. After that, he started talking to realtors and collecting floor plans for A-frame summer homes, but instead of getting closer to a cottage, my uncle and father began squabbling about vacation dates or my father realized that we didn't have enough money to buy anything like a second home, and the next summer he decided we'd vacation in Montana for two weeks, skipping Wisconsin altogether.

That was the summer between high school and college for me, the summer I was old enough to begin giving up on my father's dream and start finding my own kind of nature to define myself around. This wasn't done consciously, but when I got a job as a park ranger out West starting the summer between my junior and senior years of college, I began transferring my love for the lake of my childhood and adolescence to the mountain landscape I was employed in for seven years. Mountain lakes, of course, are always cold watered, and most of them are small and looked at more than played in or on, but my connection to them became close and my mountain identity became solidified and separate from that of my parents and brothers.

One October, four or five years after I finished college, during a period when my father and uncle were good friends again, my parents and I paid a short visit to the lake with my uncle, and I saw the island for the first time lit up in the reds and yellows of fall. The interior of the cabin was the same as I had remembered it, and all weekend as we sat at the table talking and eating, my father was still scheming about lake houses and property. His focus now, however, was on the various ways a cottage could be handed down to his children. Both days we were there, I walked alone around the island, empty of everyone else. When I came to Boathouse Bay the second day, I lay down in the grass near where I remembered one of the island kids stepping on a nail, and I smelled the heat of the autumn sun and felt the warmth of the leaves all around. It was like being tucked into bed.

Though he drafted "Once More to the Lake" many times over the years, E. B. White only wrote this one essay about his lake, an essay that any reader can tell is really about death. I felt the premonition of White's final paragraph the next time I went to the cottage, a year before my father was diagnosed with the lung cancer that killed him. It was another fall visit spent with my parents and uncle, and for some reason I kept bumping into my dim childhood memories of old-timers disappearing from the island. There was the memory of my brother and I finding shards of bones above the shore and being told that they were Mr. Fulton's "ashes" that his son had left after crossing the lake's frozen surface one winter day. There was the memory of returning in the red and green canoes and finding Colonel Finn, our neighbor to the south, dead in his rocking chair, looking as if he were reading the newspaper spread on his lap. And there was the memory of Mrs. Summers hanging out sheets and towels in the island breeze each year, until one year there was no laundry because there was no Mrs. Summers.

One afternoon, while my mother and uncle were cleaning up after lunch, my father and I set off for Indian Point in the old aluminum fishing boat. There was, he had told me, a cottage for sale that he wanted to see, but when we arrived and walked back into the thick trees, I saw that it wasn't a cottage but three cottages surrounding a larger building, all constructed in the same design. It reminded me of a southern scene, all the columns and what looked like dangling moss and the way the sunlight streaked into the clearing and painted everything pale yellow. I knew that my father had been here before, that a surgeon from Chicago brought his family here every summer during the forties and fifties and that my father played tennis with his children on grass courts beside Guth's Tavern. The main building was unlocked and still furnished, and during the next hour my father gave me a guided tour through a few scenes from his past as well as through his vision of a future I wanted to imagine but couldn't.

The next day, before leaving the lake, my father hired a realtor, and for the rest of the year until the following summer when his cancer was diagnosed, he negotiated to buy the estate on Indian Point so my brothers and I would each have a small cottage of our own surrounding one main building where we could meet together for meals. During those months both my parents often called me separately in North Carolina, my father to update me on his negotiations, my mother to update me on her concerns. She was worried that her retirement funds and a recent small inheritance from her side of the family would be invested five hundred miles away in four cottages that were falling apart. I listened to her patiently and sympathetically, but I didn't tell her that as outlandish and impractical as my father's idea was, I was on his side the whole time.

When my father was sick, I remember him saying he didn't need to go to the lake once he knew he was dying because its image was always with him. And, as it turned out, just as Mr. Fulton's ashes were brought to the island after he died, my father asked us to bring his. Only instead of crossing the lake when it was frozen like cement and leaving them above the shore as Mr. Fulton's son did, we waited until summer and motored the old fishing boat out toward the point and the deepest water. It was there my mother, brothers, and I each took a handful of the dust and handed it over to the wind.

During that trip to the island, we all stayed a week, my husband and two daughters and I volunteering to sleep at one of the neighbors' because there was no room for us in the cottage. In the mornings the adults would help the four cousins fish for crawdads from the dock or take a group walk to the backside of the island and sit on Kissing Rock. In the afternoons we'd swim when the sun was hot enough, and my youngest brother would fish for musky and pike with his son. Sometimes I'd get out the canoe, but because of a change in the lake's acidity, there weren't as many reeds to slide through as there had been when I was a kid. At least twice a day, we'd walk over to the calm side of the island to see the eagle's nest floating high in the sky. When I was young, we rarely even saw these birds soaring from a distance, but now if you stood at just the right place on the hillside, you could glimpse into their nest at feeding time and see little heads and beaks moving and dancing, waiting for their parents to return with more food. I enjoyed watching the eagles, but even more I loved watching the cousins watch nature work and I always wondered which one of them was feeling it most.

Our next visit happened a couple years later when we decided to have a family reunion that my older brother couldn't make at the last minute. My youngest brother and his family were already on the island with my mother and uncle when my husband and I flew into Milwaukee with our daughters and rented a car to drive north. As we parked in the grass beside Guth's, I saw my brother waiting to pick us up in his new red and white fiberglass speedboat. That was the summer my oldest daughter tried skiing, and my youngest daughter and I tried rowing to Guth's until a storm erupted and we turned back under black clouds. My husband didn't like the claustrophobic feeling of the island, especially with so many people under one roof, so we explored the mainland more than usual, driving to Antigo for ice cream one day and to Rhinelander for lunch another, and one afternoon we visited the little museum in Elcho and looked at black-and-white photographs of the area stored in cardboard boxes.

Mostly I remember the afternoon when I saw my brother through the thin, warped glass of the cottage's back window. He was outside talking to Tom Ebert and since it was the third of July, I imagined the two of them were discussing the picnic that was always held at noon on the Fourth in the island clubhouse, a white, square building set back from the water and only opened this one day each year. When I went out to join them, however, it wasn't the picnic that was being discussed, but the owner's meeting beforehand that only deed holders could attend. Tom was the son of a woman who was part of my father's generation, and he and I and the rest of the older kids used to walk the island's perimeter on dark nights without flashlights. Now he was a deed holder himself and president of the island association, and after a few seconds of silence, I realized that my youngest brother was now a deed holder too and that my uncle had handed down our family cottage to him and not to me or my other brother or any of the cousins I barely knew. The realization came to me fast, not through the cause and effect of logic, but through a full-bodied electrical bolt that left me burnt and then charged.

I wish I could say that when Tom Ebert left I took in this life-changing moment like a mature adult and sat down on one of the old cushioned chairs to swallow the news of my exclusion like some kind of medicine. I wish I could write that I went down on the dock or out in the canoe or to the backside of the island to get some distance between this new information and me. But I did neither. Instead, when Tom left, I felt a click inside of me like a latch being opened and my anger burst into the main room of the cottage with so much noise and energy that the cousins stopped playing their board game at the round table and my sister-in-law left through the front door. The sound everyone in the cottage heard that afternoon was a pulsing tangle of words focused on the unjust decision I felt had been made without anyone telling me a thing. The sound I heard was my heart, not beating or skipping, but being ripped from the place I loved.

No anger rears up and kicks wildly in White's "Once More to the Lake." Instead the essay continues on a steady course of nostalgic reflection and summer tranquility almost until its end. After my outburst that afternoon, the family bonded together to erase or, at least, cover up the emotion I'd unleashed. My uncle and brother stood around silent, not acknowledging that anything had happened, and my mother, as if bringing reason into the room, explained that an old cottage needs upkeep that my brother could best afford. All four cousins went back to their game. Had my husband not been standing in the room that day, I wouldn't now believe that everything had happened in the way that I remember.

Two days after I learned about the deed, my brother and uncle began hauling what they called junk out to the aluminum boat, almost as if they had been waiting for me to find out the truth so they could begin work. They brought out rusted tools and fishing gear from the shed, old linens and flat cushions from the sleeping porch, dusty cardboard boxes from somewhere, filled and heavy with I didn't know what contents. My mother seemed to condone what she saw as a long-overdue cleaning project, but I watched for as long as I could, numb and hurt, no one involving me or wondering what this fast dismantling of the past meant. When my brother brought down two metal headboards from the twin beds upstairs, I wanted to protest but didn't. When he carried out the black-and-white wool jacket from the closet, I felt something like grief. Still on its hanger, the jacket had been in the cottage for as long as I could remember. I had put it on over my own coat on cold mornings more than once, and over the years, I'd seen my father and uncle and both of my brothers wear it. No one knew who it belonged to, so I always thought, and I assumed everyone else did too, that it belonged to all of us and to the cottage in which it hung.

At least two boatloads of the cottage's possessions went over to the mainland that afternoon, and the next day my brother and uncle took down the wall separating the two rooms upstairs to make one modern living space. The following day I saw our metal headboards sticking out of the dumpster next to Guth's, and though I started scheming about ways to rescue them, in the end I did nothing. The morning before we flew back to North Carolina, wooden bunk beds and new mattresses were delivered by pontoon for the sleeping porch downstairs and my niece and nephew argued over who would get to sleep up on top. They had no idea—or maybe they did—about how I imagined what my own daughters were feeling and thinking as they looked on from their cushions arranged like beds on the floor.

It's been over eight years since that last trip to the lake. When we left, my uncle took us to the airport in Rhinelander, and I remember him simultaneously waving goodbye and mouthing "come back" as we turned to walk toward the plane. Sometimes I imagine there were tears in his eyes as he realized how much I loved this place and how hurt I felt when he chose my brother over me. Other times I think that the choice he made to give the cottage to my youngest brother, who was a physician living three hours away in Madison, was nothing more than a business decision made by a man with no heirs.

Today my mom often informs me about the lake on the phone, hinting that the cottage is a liability with its taxes and repairs and the expense of putting up the dock each winter. My oldest brother told me he doesn't mind being excluded from the deed. To him the cottage is too far from his Southern California home, and he seems content considering the lake as a magical and important but closed chapter of his past. My youngest brother still has not discussed the cottage with me, though he's recently invited my family to vacation there and started including me in the lake pictures he emails to my mother and other brother: a fish he's caught, the leaves he's raked, a sunset. It's through him that we know when more old-timers on the island have died. Last fall he phoned me for advice about the boathouse—should it be repaired or replaced—and though I'd let a lot of my anger settle and dissipate, I just didn't know how to respond.

Sometimes I think I teach "Once More to the Lake" because it's a way I can visit a place I often think about but can no longer touch. Smelling White's "wet woods" and hearing his small waves "chucking the rowboat under the chin" transport me back to my lake more than just remembering it on my own ever can. Without White, I forget about the "rusty screens" in the sleeping porch and the red squirrels on the "roof, tapping out [their] gay routine in the morning." I forget about the thin "partitions" on the second floor of the cottage and how they didn't "extend clear to the top of the rooms." I forget about the "cool nerve" it took to land the aluminum fishing boat at the dock, "shutting off the motor at the proper time and coasting in with a dead rudder." Somehow, I even forget about taking the canoe out early on still mornings, "keeping close along the shore in the long shadow of the pines" and feeling as if I were in a "cathedral." Putting that essay on my course syllabus each year is like planning for a short trip.

Whenever my classes discuss the essay's final paragraph, most students protest. Their gripe isn't with White's son grabbing his wet swimsuit from the clothesline, but the quick shift from "garment" to "groin" to "death" as he pulls it on and the way the essay leaps from the particular image of a young boy getting ready to go into the water to the universal epiphany of a father as he watches his child and is ambushed by the knowledge of his own death. This year when I taught the essay, a few students described the ending as cliché, arguing that I'd urge them to take out a phrase such as "the chill of death" if they tried using it as the last four words in their own essays. To me the ending is perfect, but because there are no grandparents or extended family anywhere in sight in White's paragraphs, it's not my ending. In other words, E. B. White would have left us with quite a different gift if his family had owned, and not rented, property on that lake.

My father's mother—the grandmother who died before my first birthday—had an older sister named Bea. According to my mom, Aunt Bea always liked my father, the black sheep of the family flock. When we were children, she sent my brothers and me Christmas money from California each year, a couple of brand new dollar bills pressed flat and stiff in special money cards that displayed George Washington's face framed in an oval. She would sign the cards simply *Bea*, and over the years that word became shaky until the cards stopped arriving and I was old enough to realize how little I knew about someone I only remember seeing once, but always sensed a presence of when I was at the lake and saw her name etched into the paneled wall along with the names of my other relatives. She had, I suspect, canoed in the same canoe that I had, reached for the same thin chain at sunset to click on the lamp hanging above the round table.

My mother once told me that Aunt Bea loved the lake, and when I look at her in photographs, I know that she did. In one picture her hair is swept off her face and she's smiling and standing in front of the cottage. In another she's holding an oar. She seems about fifteen, infused with love for a place that she probably carried into adult life. I never heard about my aunt being estranged from the family once her sister—my grandmother—was given the deed to the cottage, though I suspect something inside her shifted when that sharp decision was made. I do know that she didn't step on the island for decades and that my uncle—once he became the deed holder—only saw his mother's sister when visiting her in California.

Sometimes when I read "Once More to the Lake," I think my Aunt Bea might have thought of our lake's storms in orchestral terms the way that White does at the end of his essay, with the kettledrum rumbling and the cymbals flashing and the lightning crackling against black clouds. During daydreams such as these, I always picture my aunt in the cottage, watching the wind and the waves like lake lovers do, though after the storm passed, I doubt she would have run outside to pull her wet swimsuit from the clothesline. That didn't happen at our lake, where temperatures were too cold for swimming after a good summer rain. Instead, Aunt Bea would have stayed inside reading or fingering worn puzzle pieces the way I once did when the excitement of an island storm melted into the pleasure of having everyone in the family warm and together around the table. What I know for sure is that my aunt wouldn't have sat there wondering about her proprietary future just as I didn't think about my own when I was that age, the cottage protecting me from storms, the island and lake insulating the cottage from the world.

Driving to
Russia

⋙ ✦ ⋘

THE SUMMER we attend Russian culture camp, Marina is thirteen. Thin. Hair the color Russians call chestnut. For years I've tried to nourish my daughter with her birth country, thinking it will solidify her identity, but Russia has all but evaporated from her everyday life.

"She's not Russian," my husband always argued when I lobbied for us to attend one of the events planned by our adoption agency, "culture matters more than where she was born." I'd look at him, maybe respond, wonder how he got things so easy.

"We can't dish up Russia in the middle of North Carolina," he'd say.

I couldn't disagree, but I also couldn't help insisting that we pack the girls into their booster seats and drive thirty miles to attend the agency's annual picnic or ice cream social where we'd stand with fifty other parents we barely knew as our born-in-Russia children ate too many potato chips or drenched scoops of ice cream with chocolate and caramel sauce.

That's the way my mothering has gone since we adopted Marina: my reaching for Marina's heritage and grasping at almost nothing. What I'm really after for her is something close to what I know about myself: my English and German descent, my ancestry of midwestern farming and North Woods lumbering and small-town banking. The family stories and lore and people that help tell me who I am and where I'm from that I can pass to Tess, our biological daughter. Since Marina's ancestry is mostly an unmarked snowfield, giving her a whole country seemed like the best I could do—my attempt at strapping little snowshoes on her feet.

I first heard about culture camp the year Marina was two, and I put it on the back burner. In the meantime, Marina squirmed through adoption-agency-sponsored demonstrations of Moscow folk dancers and mutinied when the Russian ballet performed *Swan Lake* at a nearby university. She ignored our readings of Tolstoy's stories for children and the Chagall prints hanging in Kevin's office. When Tess was cast as one of Mother Ginger's *polichinelles*, Marina still could not have cared less about Tchaikovsky's *The Nutcracker*. My youngest daughter has never eaten a spoonful of borscht. Or enjoyed classes in gymnastics. Or been drawn to the sixty-by-seventy-inch framed world map hanging on one wall of her bedroom, with Russia, not the United States, displayed huge and slightly off-center like a heart.

One year I splurged on Russian Christmas ornaments sold as a fundraiser by our adoption agency. Two dozen, carved from wood and hand painted, that I imagined Marina and I slipping into plastic gift bags and tying with red and green ribbon. But when I set up the project on our dining room table, Marina played with her Legos, not even admiring the shiny eggs and smiling *matryoshkas*. When we took several ornaments to Philadelphia to give to the Russian women caring for Kevin's parents, they scooped Marina up and spoke her name like only native speakers can, but it was Tess, not Marina, who agreed to present these gifts to them. And it was Tess's arm that one caregiver, a former Soviet Olympic swim coach, lifted up and admired.

"You—big—muscles," she said, announcing that our oldest daughter should be a competitive swimmer.

By the time Marina was five or six, our attendance at adoption agency events had trickled down to the annual Father Frost Festival, the Russian Christmas celebration that reemerged in the early nineties thanks to the rise of democracy and capitalism. After that, I don't know whether I let go of the agency or the agency let go of me, but we stopped making the effort and the parting seemed mutual. No one in my family ever seemed to miss the January seventh celebration featuring a tall man with his long, white beard and robes of blue and white. The last Father Frost celebration we attended I went alone with the girls, and I remember having a headache. Too many kids were running around the hall of a church and too much food, not necessarily Russian, overflowed from paper plates. Father Frost looked shabby that year, like he really had emerged from the woods he was purported to live in, and whatever magic was there for the girls in the past was gone. By then Marina had learned that the man she probably thought of as the blue Santa Claus was good for one tiny gift while the real guy in red, who came down the chimney thirteen days earlier, was good for many more.

It was about that time I started perusing the culture camp brochures I'd requested a couple years before. It seemed unlikely that traveling all the way to Colorado was a better way to get to Russia, but the campers in the photographs looked happy.

"And," I told Kevin when first introducing the option, "we'd be with a 'sea of families' just like ours."

My husband looked at me as if I had finally and thoroughly lost my mind. "I'm quoting from the brochure," I said.

A big obstacle with camp for us, besides its cost and location almost two thousand miles west from our home, was that family members had to attend together, an idea that never gelled when we were making vacation plans, especially as the girls got older.

The last time I brought up the idea at dinner, it flopped. "Mom," Tess said, "you're kidding, right?" Marina's answer was succinct. "I'm not going," she said.

So even I'm surprised one July afternoon when I find myself driving a rental car up into the Rockies with my travel-loving mother beside me and Marina in the back seat listening to her iPod while Kevin stays behind in North Carolina to take care of Tess. We're in elk country, and it comforts me to realize that elk also live in Siberia close to where Marina is from. Although I'm not really expecting Russia in the midst of all this Colorado beauty, it does seem wrong when the valley opens up and camp appears as a group of dark-brown log buildings surrounded by a split rail fence.

At our first camp dinner, we sit alone at a round table with plates of mashed potatoes and salad and bread still corralled on our cafeteria trays. I find myself observing the other children, looking for some indication of what they have in common with my daughter.

"That kid looks your age," I say to Marina, nodding to a grey T-shirted girl sitting with parents I wouldn't mind talking to, but Marina's face slides into what I've come to think of as her typical, disinterested teenage expression. My mother reads over the camp schedule divided into separate events for parents and children and earmarks the events she wants to attend.

"Ukrainian egg decorating sounds interesting," she says. "I might try that."

"What about you?" I ask Marina.

"Archery," she says, knowing that target practice is not part of the agenda, but that because our camp is held within a bigger camp, which hosts family reunions all summer, we can take part in typical camp activities, but on our own time, at our own expense.

"Why don't you go with the middle school kids in the morning," I say, "and I'll take you to archery after lunch." It's a compromise that semi-works. When I pick Marina up after her first session, she has painted an orange bird on a small canvas with oils, but it's clear that she's connecting with none of the other children or with the counselors who are college-age volunteers. Usually social at school, if not with the kids then with the teachers, Marina walks over to me silent, no one noticing that she's leaving the group, but when we're alone we have fun shooting arrows into targets and vinyl-coated polyester statues of wildlife: a deer, a bear, a brontosaurus.

"How was the session this morning?" I ask, loading up an arrow, holding it steady, drawing back my elbow as Marina watches, tells me to reposition my feet. "What did the counselors talk about?"

That's what the three of us do the four days we're here: stumble through our own little camp within a camp, sticking primarily to ourselves and negotiating every move, but not quite fully participating. If Marina goes to the session about how kids can make a difference in the world, I'll take her horseback riding later. If my mother attends a beet salad demonstration, she'll take Marina on a hike and I'll attend a session on the rewards of parenting an adopted child. When I suggest we attend "Finding Your International Birth Mother" together, as a team, Marina refuses to accompany me and asks to go swimming.

With our camp-within-a-camp plan, none of us seems angry or frustrated or feeling as if we're wasting our time or money. Instead we're interested campers, watching what's happening to others even when we're right there participating: waving the Russian flag with one hand and the American flag with the other; learning steps to a Russian folk dance we'll never dance again; following along at the end of the opening ceremony parade, some parent's gymnastic prodigy doing back handsprings in front of us like a mechanical toy.

A vodka tasting and silent auction are scheduled for the last night of camp. My mother and I try orange and lemon vodka, and then discuss their differences. Each taste is five dollars, served in little paper thimbles smaller than the Dixie cups I once drank Kool-Aid from. We sit at a round table with other mothers. Most of them single, not just at camp, but when they return home. I've only met one other mother who, like me, is attending camp without her spouse.

Marina sits glum beside me with roller skates tied on to her feet. The rest of the kids are skating in a makeshift rink, going around counterclockwise, and even though I know I'm being ridiculous, I imagine her joining them and rewinding time, meeting the Russian-born friend she's never had, getting a closer connection to where she's from.

"Don't you want to skate?" I ask more than once, and when she finally stands I have the urge to push her gently into the rink. Instead Marina rolls off toward a line of tables stretched along one wall.

Like the vodka tasting, the silent auction is part social event and part fundraiser. The whole camp, I've discovered, is dual purposed, functioning to educate and entertain campers and to generate income and gather donations. What I've come to understand and accept is that adoptive parents are a major part of the scaffolding that keeps the institution of Russian adoption standing in the early years of the twenty-first century. Besides bringing our own possessions to camp, we were asked to bring winter clothes to be sent to an orphanage in Putvil, Ukraine, and Russian toys and crafts to replenish the camp's cultural treasure chest. As a family of a middle school camper, we were also assigned "spa items" for the silent auction. Some parents' camp job was to arrange lotions and shower gels and soaps into one huge gift basket for parents to bid on.

At a distance, I've been watching Marina glide from item to item, checking out possibilities. It's my mother who keeps conversation going at the table, skaters circling around and squealing behind her, the other mothers looking tired, and I don't doubt that they are. I'm half in the conversation, half with my daughter who is rolling our way. My prediction: she'll want the movie night gift basket packed with popcorn and DVDs donated by families with preschoolers through second graders. Instead she takes my hand and leads me to the right side of the tables, stopping in front of a plump and folded sweatshirt, the kind that's pulled over your head. Bright white, like a cloud. Like snow. Siberian.

"Is this something you want?" I ask, knowing my daughter well enough to know that it is and the question I've just asked has been scripted between us.

Marina nods, and I hold up the sweatshirt. Unfurl it. On its front, the words "Russian Fairytales & Folklore" below an orange bird spreading its embroidered wings. It's the firebird, the magical creature with feathers of flames that I recognize as similar to the bird Marina painted during her first camp session.

In Russian folklore, the firebird is both blessing and curse to its captor: a blessing because whoever sets out to capture it becomes a hero, a curse because the task is not easy. The second day of camp, I attended a lecture given by a university professor who explained that the quest for the bird is usually initiated by whoever finds one of its lost tail feathers. Since the firebird is this year's camp theme, each child was given a bright-reddish feather during the opening night ceremonies, one of which I found under a folding chair the next day. Although the professor was knowledgeable and her lecture was well attended, the session made me wonder about this bird. Was it supposed to represent Russia? Was its story meant to parallel the difficult life of the adoptee? Did its capture represent adoption? Were Kevin and I, according to the legend, captors?

"It's a pretty big sweatshirt," I say, holding it up to my daughter. Size large, adult, it hangs down to her knees. I scan the tables, looking for other, maybe smaller, child-size sweatshirts. "But I can see why you like it."

Her choice seems enigmatic—a huge sweatshirt emblazoned with signs of a camp she has rejected, but I know her focus won't veer to any other item. "Should we raise the bid two dollars?" I ask, pointing to the bidding sheet. I watch my daughter print tiny block letters next to our offering, then I join my mother, and the two of us table shop, leaving Marina behind on her roller skates to keep guard.

For the next thirty minutes before bidding closes, Marina summons me over from wherever I'm standing. Our $27 counterbid becomes $52, then $77, then $102. And when I check out the bidding sheet, I see the game we're playing: auction-tennis, a match of two bidders having the same goal and strategizing their best moves to get what they want. But I have no idea which person in the huge room belongs to the rollercoaster signature of our opponent. It feels as if Marina and I are lobbing our two dollar raises back to no one, trying to figure out the backhand of a ghost.

"We can't go any higher," I say. Marina turns and looks at me, her face melting, dripping onto my heart.

Ten minutes later, the auction finishes with a bell and the slow calling of names as the winners exchange their cash or check for prizes. My mother has won a professionally painted Ukrainian egg. The giant gift baskets are claimed. Because Marina and I both assume our last bid was blocked by the mystery bidder we've been competing against, the announcement of my daughter's name above all the talking and noise seems impossible. I watch Marina skate to the winner's table, then zoom back smiling. "I've won," she announces.

As I make out a check, I have a chance to look at the bidding sheet. Right under "Marina Boyle," an adult signature has been crossed out with a thick black line. As I try to make sense of our win, I feel a woman watching me and look up at her with both confusion and understanding. Even before she speaks, I'm sure she has played a role in my daughter's happiness.

"I could tell how much she wanted it," she explains. "My daughter didn't even know I was bidding."

A few minutes later, Marina stands beside me cradling her white sweatshirt.

"Why did you want this so much?" I ask her.

I'm not sure what answer I expect or want or that I'm going to get one this last night of camp—or ever. I'm not sure that I should know my daughter's secret desires, including those about sweatshirts. I'm not even sure this snowy possession will make my daughter happy or if there's a way for any of us to understand and articulate our needs. But Marina comes close. "It's for the kids at school," she says. "I want them to know where I'm from."

My Father and I Take a Vacation

—※—

I'M IN MY MID-TWENTIES when my father and I drive across the ice. It's night. March. And I'm not sure that driving to an island in a car is ever a good idea, but I don't argue. I'm holding on to the door handle with both hands because I've been instructed to keep my door slightly ajar.

"Just in case," my father says.

His door is slightly ajar too. He's gripping the handle with his left hand while steering the car with his right. The tires move over the ice like they move over snow or dirt or even pavement, but I don't trust slick surfaces or ones that are susceptible to what I imagine is sudden change. Warmth from the heater radiates from the front vents and then disappears into nothing. I feel confused and regretful and nervous. Why am I subjecting myself to northern Wisconsin with my father? I know that out there in front of me is the small island we're headed to, but all I can see is white nothing that stretches on past the beams of our headlights.

We're taking this chance, not because we don't know the risk. "I wouldn't do it," the bartender at Guth's had said as we were finishing dinner at his lakeside tavern. We're going because my father likes danger, and I've always been a good daughter who has found herself along for the ride.

∞

In the morning I wake up early. For a few seconds, I can tell I am listening for the sound of waves licking the shore. That's what you hear on this porch in summer when all the windows are open—that and the monotone buzz of fishing boats going about their work. Now everything outside is silent, and it must be too early for snowmobiles. In the next room, my father opens the door of the woodburning stove and pokes around the fire more than it needs to be tended. He's good at burning things. Not just logs but bridges to what can save him. I'm starting to figure that out, but I don't know why his moods swing back and forth like a pendulum for no reason or how they start or how I can get the really bad ones to stop. When I was a kid, the sounds of him tending the stove were comforting. My brothers and I would hear him when we woke up, when we were rolling log-like from one pushed-together bed to another, laughing and goofing around. Steamroller, we called the game, until one of us had to pee and the fun ended. That was before indoor plumbing when you had to walk all the way back to the outhouse, and by the time you did you felt the pull of the lake and its adventures and were up for the day.

When I get out of bed, I feel colder than I ever have in this cottage. I'm dressed in the flannel and fleece I slept in. Mountain clothes—ones I need in Colorado where I live now. I pull on my Sorrel boots. Slip on a down vest. If there's any life in this frozen air, I can't smell it. In the main room where my father sits staring at the stove, all the windows are boarded up and all the couches and stuffed chairs are draped with sheets. This place I love looks haunted, and in a way, it is. Not with anonymous ghosts walking through walls and whizzing around in curlicues, but with the ghosts of my ancestors—a grandmother and grandfather I never knew who brought their four sons to this cottage every summer of their childhoods for three months. I think that's why we're here, in a way—not because my father wants to see the cottage off-season like he told me he did, but because he's hoping somehow to confront a past that's spooked him.

Outside, I imagine, it's overcast. Inside, the cottage presses down on my father like an anvil, squeezing out all the charming aspects of his personality that were in play yesterday morning when we started driving. He's wearing two wool jackets, and his face is a pattern of deep lines I can feel on the tips of my fingers without touching. He won't be talking much today. He'll be going through the motions of eating and walking and breathing, and his eyes will be empty and glazed. A cigarette burns in the ashtray beside him. It's his best friend, especially when scaling whatever it is that's looming right there in the room. My role is what it's always been: to throw him a belay line and hold steady, to tell him that he's been a good father, even when I don't know whether that's true.

The question is not how to do this. I'm old enough now to realize that I'm an expert at being there for my father in a way that my brothers haven't seemed to be for years. Before I could walk, my mother tells me, I'd stand on the floor of the passenger's seat with my tiny hands on the dashboard while he drove—and in many ways I'm still standing and still trying to help.

The question now is whether I should be. A twenty-four-year-old figuring out her own life has no business trying to make an unhappy man happy, especially one who often lashes out with rage at his family and doesn't really understand that he has. "It would be better for all of you," my father told me a couple years ago as he drew his signature three-dimensional arrows pointing every which way on a napkin during lunch, "if I were an alcoholic." At the time I didn't understand the connection he was making between his behavior and a serious addiction, and it seemed wrong. But I'm starting to think he might have told me something important. My father's obsession with dissecting his past and the faults in his character is a kind of disease. It doesn't always look that bad from the outside—he never stumbles or slurs sentences or blacks out. There are no hidden bottles of booze. But his long periods of silence punctuated with bursts of rage are destructive, and he's lost jobs and friendships and opportunities because of them. Now that I've been on my own for half a decade, I'm starting to understand that all fathers don't operate in the world like mine does.

◇◇◇

There's no law that you can't come to this island off-season, but few people do. The islanders here are summer vacationers who like the buoyancy of water, and most of the cottages aren't winterized. After breakfast I decide to set off on the snowy trail circling the perimeter of the island.

"Dad . . . " I say at the door, feeling as if I must ask my father along, but knowing—even before I do—that he'll ignore me.

Outside it's cold, but I wish it were even colder. The VW Beetle that has stranded me here sits beached, looking whale-like on the ice, and I still don't trust water that can hold up the weight of a car.

In Colorado, winter is risky because the mountainous terrain is more vertical than horizontal. Without the incline, snowfields and glaciers wouldn't be that dangerous, and, of course, avalanches wouldn't occur. Blizzards and whiteouts and postholing take on more serious dimensions when the ground isn't flat. The landscape in Wisconsin, by contrast, is easy to negotiate, and except for my ignorance about how and when lakes change form and my knowledge that even cars can drown, the natural world surrounding me seems clear and safe. The snow is beautiful, and I love all of the white. Birch trees play hide-and-seek, and the sounds of blue jays and a lone hammering woodpecker touch my soul and fill me up. This is the kind of landscape I'm most familiar with from my childhood, but I'm not sure it would comfort me now without my years working as a backcountry ranger in the mountains. The mountains have taught me about hypothermia and silence and crampons. I've slept in snow caves and searched for snow-buried bodies with a probe. I know storm clouds and when to wait them out. More than once I've skied at midnight under the light of a pulsing round moon. There is, I suspect now as I move along the trail, a way that nature can make you strong enough to survive a father like mine.

∞∞

This island we're on is shaped like an arrowhead. Eighteen cottages dot its sharp edges like pearls on a necklace, and the short side where the clasp would be set is too marshy for building. Most of the cottages have been handed down through family members for generations, and most come with stories I can open up and read just by looking at their snow-covered doorsteps as I pass. Some are suspenseful but end happily. Mr. Ludwig, for example, was rescued one night when he fell overboard while trolling for fish.

But other stories that survive are mysterious and sometimes tragic. Divorces and drowning and murder can happen to island people in Milwaukee and Minneapolis and Michigan, and once they do, the details of what happened are absorbed deep into the wood and windows and roofs of the cottages and can't easily be rubbed out. There's the story that Mr. Dillinger hanged himself and that's why no one ever stays at his cottage and its porch has rotted away. And there's the story about the Babses and the Dodges, next-door neighbors on the island who became bedfellows when Mr. Dodge started sleeping with Mrs. Babs and Mr. Babs started sleeping with Mrs. Dodge.

The past rises to the surface in winter when there are no distractions, when someone isn't waving to you from their dock or passing you on the trail or looking for blueberries at the same place you planned to pick. In summer, life on the island is busy and full. Sometimes, though, when I was a kid, night scared me, like when I returned from taking the boat to the boathouse by myself and heard a sound I didn't know, or when I was a teenager and a couple of us would walk around the island after we assumed everyone was asleep. Without a moon, nights on the island are a beautiful shade of black and stars sparkle like glitter, but I never wanted to be the last teenager in line. It wasn't too scary on the arrowhead sides of the island, but past the Eberts, when the trail veers away from the lake and into the marsh, my laughing and chattering always softened to whispers. The terrain wasn't what I was nervous about or the bats or the dense underbrush. I was afraid of something from the past pulling me somewhere I'd never been, somewhere I didn't want to be.

As kids we always seemed to navigate the island counterclockwise, but today, without realizing it, I'm moving in the other direction, and nothing looks like itself. The lake is a long sheet of paper that reminds me of desert or prairie without grass. Far out beside Treacherous Bay, tiny specks might be ice fishermen looking for their luck in a hole. Water has become land, but once I've circled the entire island and stand in front of our cottage again, I no longer sense the awe of nature as much as I feel disorientated and anxious, pulled back to where I started because what other choice do I have? My father's smoke from the woodstove still curls from the concrete chimney. There is no wind. Except for a slideshow of memories looping through my brain, the row of boarded-up windows in front of me is a blank page that I realize I'm trying to read.

I like to imagine that before electricity arrived on the island, life each summer might have been like camping, and my father might have enjoyed walking to the community icehouse each morning to get ice for his family's perishable food. I do know that when my father was about ten, Leonard Guth taught him the art of paddling a canoe and that someone shot through the fishline instead of through the musky's head when my grandfather caught his first fish and that one summer's night my grandmother fell into the hole in the outhouse and had to keep yelling for help. When my father told me these stories, though, I never knew what they were supposed to mean, and I still don't. I always had the sense that they might not even be real, that they might be covering up the past and that there might be other stories my father wasn't telling me, and these were the ones that matter, the ones I still need to hear.

∞

The next morning when we pack up, it's early. Neither of us mentions the warmth in the cottage or worries out loud about how high the temperature must rise before it's able to change the form of a lake. My father wears only one jacket as he shovels ash from the belly of the stove with a concentration I know well. I'm pretty sure that outside it's *socked in*—an expression I learned in the mountains to talk more accurately about the weather.

In summer, departures from the island are a production. Someone has to strip the beds and haul the sheets and towels to and from the laundromat in Elcho while someone stays behind to clean, but my father and I pull up stakes easily in winter: washing nothing but dishes, folding the used linens back up and placing them just where they were in the center of the beds as if no one has been here. We haven't even been upstairs. I scrape off our leftover dinner from the plates, watch my father move in slow motion as he places yellowed copies of the *Milwaukee Journal* back into the kindling box. He's smoking again, still in another world no one but he can enter.

Because you don't have to worry about waves getting you wet, it turns out crossing to the mainland by car is easier than by boat. Without saying a word, we simply stow our suitcases and trash in the trunk and take our places in the front seat. Above us, the sky is a single cloud. In front of us, the cottage is framed in the windshield like a nineteenth-century painting. As my father backs up and points the car in the direction we're headed, the distant shoreline comes into view as a long abstract line. I turn toward my father's profile, wanting to say something and then changing my mind. Somewhere out there this lake is thirty-nine feet deep; we've already backed up onto depths that are over our heads.

Over the years I've grown up assuming that my ancestors were well respected both on and off the island. My grandfather was president of a small-town bank. All of his sons, except my father, ended up as presidents of small-town banks too. And the story I've always told myself was this: that my father, the artist of the bunch, who supported his wife and three children as a photographer, wasn't a black sheep as much as he was a shiny gem—the son with the talent. Driving across the ice, however, after spending two days alone with my father in the cottage for the first time, I'm not so sure that the past was what I, or anyone from the outside, might have thought it was. Who were these relatives of mine that my father lived with when he was a boy? What kind of complicated and troubled relationship did he have with his parents? Why does this man who gave me life often disappear into silence as dark as death?

Maybe because it's broad daylight or because the whole lake is empty or because rain starts bearing down on the windshield like tiny knives, I finally understand my father is someone with secrets I can't save. For a long instant, this knowledge doesn't seem like much, but then I realize it might be everything, and I feel lighter, as if I'm hovering over the ice. Beside me my father still sits driving with his hands on the steering wheel. Below us I imagine walleyes and bass and northern pike, not frozen in place in mid-swim, but lying low in the oxygen-deprived dark at the bottom of the lake, most of them surviving until spring. That's when Guth's comes into clear view like a tiny anchor, and I know our little car will make it across the ice and pull up onshore like some kind of odd amphibious vehicle. It will probably be raining harder by then, and my father will keep the motor running as, stoop-shouldered and sad, he transfers our trash from the trunk to the dumpster.

After that he'll turn left out of Guth's parking lot and take to the wet highway, and I'll realize that he's driving too fast, the windshield wipers going back and forth as if they are slapping the glass. At that point my heart will acknowledge the weight that has been handed down to me. It's a weight that could crack any surface, still pull me under.

Oxford Through the
Looking Glass

⟳ ✦ ⟲

In Oxford there is almost nothing you cannot learn.

—Jan Morris

MOST PEOPLE, myself included, like to map the past against the present. Virginia Woolf does this kind of mapping in *To the Lighthouse*, a novel always worth returning to. Willa Cather does it in *My Ántonia*. It's a technique as familiar as breath, as old as the *Odyssey*. Like tenacious investigators we search out the same smells, sounds, sights, scenes, even moments of sadness that we've known, but what we're really looking for is evidence of ourselves, clues that we've been somewhere before where something happened and confirmation that we've found ourselves in that same place again.

For me, a crucial revelation about my Oxford existence occurred when I was standing at the curb facing the basement flat on Norham Road where I'd lived thirty years before with a man named Dan. As is often the case, all the makings of this revelation had been within my reach for some years, but it took being at what I now think of as a site of personal tragedy for the magic of insight to gel, for the molecules to begin bonding together, forming a shape I recognized immediately as understanding.

It was a cold afternoon when this happened, when I finally processed what others had been telling me for years and moved beyond acceptance to revelation and then knowledge. Most likely, it wasn't coincidental that this revelation occurred with me bookended by my husband, Kevin, and our twenty-two-year-old daughter, Tess. The three of us had been in Oxford for less than a week, Tess arriving from Madrid where she was teaching English for a year, and Kevin and I arriving for a semester of teaching and writing associated with one of our university's study abroad programs. Before we'd made our way to Norham Road that afternoon, we'd been touring the heart of the city on foot, Kevin soaking in the smorgasbord of history and geography spread out in front of him, Tess asking to see Christ Church with its great hall and the staircase leading up to it, both of which have ties to the Harry Potter films she had grown up with. For me, exploring here and there while wrapped in wool and layered in puffy down was more complicated than the simple joy of seeing something new.

There were the sporadic, whirring moments of getting my bearings, of mistaking the roundness of the Sheldonian

Theatre for the Radcliffe Camera, of remembering whether Broad Street was High Street or the reverse, of sensing the scale of a town that was smaller in reality than it had been all those years in my imaginings.

More than that were the ghosts chasing me down. Everywhere we went was a kind of haunting. At Brasenose College, I had once taught high school students for one month. At Blackwell's Bookstore, I had once watched one of Dan's friends working the cash register. At the pub on the corner, I'd sat outside more than once drinking half pints of beer in the summer sun. I'd already been past the Turf, the Bear, and the Bodleian many times before. I'd already walked under the Bridge of Sighs where my daughter wanted to take photographs, gotten up close against this city that was going to be my home again for another six months. The whole day that Kevin and Tess and I were dodging pedestrians, I felt as if I would bump into the past like an old acquaintance I wasn't sure I wanted to see. I also felt that something or someone was watching me from somewhere I couldn't know, measuring me and sizing me up, deciding whether I had changed in the past three decades and become wiser, or not.

What I began realizing earlier that morning when I'd brought up my first life in Oxford to my husband and daughter is that no matter how much I was interested in my past and the insight it gave me, no one else was, not even two of the people closest to me. And why should they be? When the 6A bus we took from our university's flat passed Norham

Road for the first time on our way to the city center, shivers that had nothing to do with the damp British cold crept up my back, but I didn't know what to say. That's where I used to live with another man in another life? That's the place where he told me he no longer loved me?

When I finally did point out the road, identified by its long, thin, rectangular sign, my daughter looked up from her phone and my husband followed my finger and nodded. They were polite. It's not that they didn't care. They did to some extent, enough even to humor me and stand at the curb in what had been one of the most prestigious Oxford neighborhoods all the way back to the nineteenth century.

For me the experience of being at the curb that day was, at first, only disorienting in the way that something is when it is the same but different and you don't know quite why. I wasn't even sure I had led Kevin and Tess to the correct spot. Four almost identical stone houses, all semidetached and semi-Gothic, stood in a row on the north side of Norham Road, but I didn't know which one was really *it*. None of their addresses sounded familiar. Beyond that, all four were larger than I remembered, and looked heavier. At first I thought it might be the weight of the bigger cars parked in their gravel drives or their more substantial front doors painted in daring twenty-first-century colors. But when I imagined scenes from my life there, imagined going in or out of the flat or imagined walking my secondhand bike to or from the door to the street, I realized the shapes of the houses seemed different, and I wondered whether the porches and garages had been added onto the sides where I had remembered only entryways. Standing and looking at the beige stone structures and remembering them from the past reminded me of the kids' game with two identical pictures printed side by side, only the pictures weren't identical and that was the game—to discover the differences between them.

Ironically, when I looked in the windows of a basement flat that could have been mine, I saw nothing except darkness, but everything inside the flat, preserved in my memory, was just as I had left it, only it was warmer and not winter. There I was at twenty-eight just arrived in Oxford with three pieces of luggage and long hair. There Dan wore a tweed suit coat and spoke with hints of a new accent as if he'd been invaded by everything British.

And there was the bulk of a barrier between us. The same one that had been present several hours earlier when Dan had picked me up at Heathrow and I knew something was wrong, the same one that had followed us onto the train where Dan read *The Wind in the Willows* and, facing him, I stared all the way to Oxford at the cover of a children's book I'd never heard of. That same barrier became a permanent fixture in the flat, beginning that first night Dan broke up our relationship, telling me he no longer loved me.

Back then, after I'd finished my MA in fiction writing at the University of Colorado and decided to follow a man I loved across the Atlantic, I knew close to nothing about Oxford. I didn't understand the British university system, and I hadn't cared enough to research it before arriving. I hadn't brought along a city map. I hadn't thought to make a list of possible escape routes or exits. I'd simply arrived in town as if I'd jumped down a rabbit hole.

Kevin knew the story about Dan, and Tess knew an abbreviated version. She knew that her mother had been in a relationship with a theoretical chemist who went to Oxford for a postdoc, and she knew that the relationship had ended. But she didn't know *when*. Of the few unresolved mysteries from my twenties, chief among them is not why I went to Oxford to live with my boyfriend, Dan, but why I stayed and lived with him for more than six months once I realized the relationship was over. That had been the source of my confusion for years. Not that Dan had described his British life to me for months during late-night, international phone calls and in long letters written on thin blue airmail stationery, the kind that can be licked closed to make an envelope. Not that we had been together for three years before he left for England and bought me a one-way ticket from Denver to London as a birthday present that arrived in my hands through the regular mail. Not, even, that I ripped myself from the mountains I loved and traveled five thousand miles away to live with a man who ended up wanting to just be my friend. The tragedy was that we stayed in that flat from the beginning of June until almost Christmas living as brother and sister. The protagonist was me, tamping down my numbness and pain, and pretending as if I were fine with the situation Dan had defined for us.

Hope is a strange thing when mixed with love. I see now that all those weeks and months Dan and I lived together, I was counting on him to click back into my life so that it could return to what it had been in Colorado. From the distance of so many years, my stubborn patience and the situation I found myself in seemed unreal, but while it was happening, it was all I had. Of course, I was scared. And more emotionally injured than I knew. But I was also an expert at silence and keeping secrets.

Except for one unanswered letter I wrote to one of Dan's friends describing the breakup, I covered up what had happened, what was happening, and told no one. During those months, not even Dan and I talked about our relationship ending. I have no memory of crying.

What I do remember, with more detail than I remember yesterday, is waking up alone in the flat that first morning with loneliness and shock in my gut. Two tall, curtained windows looked out onto a back garden where it was sunny and green, and it took a few moments of just standing there to reconcile the emptiness I felt with my pleasant surroundings. Mostly, I remember walking, not the kind of walking where you orient yourself with the goal of reaching a destination. But the kind where your emotions exist in one realm and your body in another and you move through lanes and streets and alleys because that's all you can do.

Norham Road runs perpendicular to Banbury Road, and although I didn't know it then, Banbury Road is one of north Oxford's main thoroughfares leading, as the British say, into the city center. That's the direction I headed when, without thought or consideration, I turned left. That day I know I would have passed Martyrs' Memorial just after Woodstock Road merges with Banbury to become St. Giles, but after that there are so many colleges and towers and walls, so many ways to move through more than one thousand years of architectural time. Almost every building I passed that afternoon would have been the color of toast. When I looked up, I would have seen toast-colored spires and chimneys and domes. Toast-colored statues would have been on the tops of some of the buildings. Toast-colored gargoyles and grotesques circling right below the summits of others.

Over the days, my walking continued. I remember circling the shops in Oxford's Covered Market, walking past hanging pig heads and leather belts. I remember sauntering down the straightaways past colleges with names I couldn't keep straight or always pronounce. Even the colleges with names I was sure of both attracted and intimidated me with their rectangular green courtyards I could peer into but not enter. I felt this way about all of Oxford, pulled towards its knowledge that seemed almost glamourous to me and simultaneously pushed away from the same: from its powerful male past and purposeful students, from Dan's world of thermodynamics and equations, from his Oxbridge friends with their pedigrees and intelligent British accents.

One weekend one of those friends invited five of us to his parents' house, a sprawling English manor southeast of Oxford with tennis courts and a fountain and trails that wandered through meadows and over turnstiles. Saturday afternoon, everyone but me slipped on wellies for a long walk before tea. As the others moseyed along with the friend's parents in groups of two and three talking about air traffic and its infringement on British country life, I ended up behind them stepping around puddles in the cheap canvas booties I'd managed to find at a flea market.

Luckily, by the end of my first week on Norham Road, I had discovered escape hatches on either side of the city. To the east of the flat, University Park with its trees and gardens and cricket grounds lay freshly manicured, but I usually defaulted to the wilder side of nature on the west accessed through North Parade Avenue, a row of shops and two pubs. This second side of nature was Port Meadow, much further from the flat than University Park. Each time I went there, the urban landscape of houses and streets opened up to its beauty and I was almost saved. I'd walk the trail along the Thames to the south toward Oxford's train station or to the north toward Wolvercote past the spot where Lewis Carroll told some of the first *Alice in Wonderland* stories. And then I'd walk back. Long, thin river boats were always moored around Binsey. Thinner boats with their teams of scullers slid by me without a sound. Sometimes a coxswain gave directions in an English I couldn't quite make out. I remember it being sunny on Port Meadow in June. I liked the heat, the signs of life. I liked getting as much distance as possible between me and the city. I liked that this meadow had never been plowed. Horses grazed on it and cows. Ducks lingered. Port Meadow became my touchstone. My closest friend. Time by the river felt preserved. Air sweet. Colors bright.

On some of these walks, I abandoned the trails and wove in and out of the grass. One afternoon, I remember turning and glimpsing the kind of scene that J. M. W. Turner would want to paint. There were several dark horses grazing in the foreground with a couple of vertical stretches of dark trees behind them. Behind the trees, where sky and land met, Oxford was a horizontal line with tiny mountain-like spires. And behind the line, more cloud-filled sky. It was only from this vantage point that I felt the full soul of this new place I was living and could let it embrace me.

The British have a talent for walking and a love for open space that I shared with them. There were always other brave wanderers meandering along in the almost-mud of the lowlands or walking their dogs. Most days I'd pass oil painters who had set up their easels and were working. In many ways, I was out there working as well, not on art but on pain, though the two often merge. How, I wondered, had I gotten myself to a meadow in a country where I knew no one except the person who had abandoned me? What had I not let myself see?

When I knew for certain that Kevin and I would be headed to Oxford and memories of my first life there kept reappearing in ways they hadn't before, I realized I'd never really heard or believed my close friends after I'd returned to Colorado and told them what had happened, after they'd described my first life in Oxford as *impossible* or *harrowing* or *fucked up*. For years I'd thought staying with Dan was not just normal but also noteworthy, indicative of some important inner strength I possessed. It was Kevin, with his knowledge of the facts and insight into me and my life, who helped me to understand my relationship with Dan when the topic emerged and then stalled in our kitchen a week before the two of us departed for England.

"You just had a bad experience," Kevin said, zooming to the truth as if peering through the lens of a microscope and adjusting it into clear focus. "But it was weird."

"It was?" I asked, surprised at his revelation and then surprised that he was surprised that I was.

"Yes," he said.

By the time I stood surveying the scene with Kevin and Tess on Norham Road a couple months later, I had not only absorbed my husband's words as truth, but I'd also realized I'd probably stayed so long in Oxford with Dan because that's what I thought I was supposed to do. It was the model of romantic relationships I'd grown up with, especially during the four years that my father lived separate from my mother, my bothers, and me, and my mother instructed us to keep this living arrangement secret from everyone, even—it seemed—from ourselves. Women, I thought through this example, waited for men to work out whatever problem or dream they needed to. And they did it without complaint, pretending as if they didn't care. Like pillars. When my father surprised all four of us by coming back home the summer before my senior year of high school, his reentry into the family was as fluid as water. Neither of my parents discussed his reappearance with my brothers and me any more than they talked about the evening he left, backing out of the driveway and waving.

Kevin, Tess, and I didn't stay long at the curb. It was too cold, and there were other places to go. But with my arms touching theirs through layers of coats and sweaters, I looked through the past into the window for another moment at what neither my husband nor daughter could see. The overhead light glared above Dan as he walked into his room, clicking the door closed behind him like a barricade. After he'd left, I watched the woman who was me walk into what was supposed to be my room and eye the thin, cold bed pressed up against the wall. That's when I walked back out and over to the couch, pulling off its heavy cushions and making a new bed for myself so that Dan would have to step over me while I slept to get to the kitchen or front stoop.

Until that cold January afternoon, I'd always thought my nightly ritual of making a bed out of cushions and refusing to sleep where Dan wanted me to sleep was a strong act of defiance. But standing at the curb with my daughter and husband beside me and remembering all those nights on the floor, I felt a twinge of shame and saw my strange bivouac as the painful ritual it was.

If I could have, I would have stepped through all the years and into that apartment. I would have grabbed that twenty-eight-year-old me and walked out the door.

Visiting the Iditarod Champ

〜❖〜

WHEN I WAS INTRODUCED to Dwayne, he didn't seem to see me, and he definitely didn't shake my hand. His gaze was already stuck on the three young women enrolled in the course I was teaching, the women out in his yard moving among his huskies, the women he would eventually compromise. I should have counted them—not the young women—but the dogs, each roped to its own pole in the Alaska dirt, each with its own shack of a house beside its pole. For most of any day, their worlds were as big as the lengths of rope tied from their poles to their collars—the lengths allowing them to go around and around clockwise or counterclockwise, like circus animals, beside their neighbors without quite touching them. Once a day—I learned this later—handlers took them out for a run, but there must have been fifty dogs and two handlers, and I kept my distance from the frantic canine energy in front of me, remembering my father's rule about not approaching strange dogs.

But the three young women in the course didn't have my kind of father, and they zoomed right up to the dogs, putting their young faces beside the muzzles of these almost wild animals and loving them, hugging them, calling them each by the name painted sloppily in blue above most of the doghouse doors. The whole scene was—well—astounding, and because I felt sorry for the dogs, I eventually moved cautiously into a few of their little orbits and gave them attention, maybe a pat on the head, and I realized that the male students, Patrick and Willie, and even Joe, my coteacher, were following my lead. Dwayne was ignoring them too and bouncing back and forth like a pinball between the three beautiful women answering this question and that, and all of a sudden I knew what he would be like out in a bar. "Hello, I'm Dwayne," he'd say leaning over his beer. "Do you want to come over and see my dogs?" Something like that.

At this point we were halfway through the fourteen-day course, and over and over again, Joe had taken us places so that we stumbled upon not just Alaska, but Alaskans. An Athabascan woman who demonstrated how to harvest wild celery with one sharp pull of its stalk. A high school math teacher who worked a fish camp each summer. A Russian Orthodox priest. Just that morning a young man named Josh showed us a documentary of a local dogsled race and mentioned that he'd participated. Not as a racer, but as a guide for a woman from Germany—and this just got me—who was legally blind. So far, I realized, my first experience teaching in Alaska had been anything but dishonorable. Even the drunk I saw when I picked up the key to the public showers at the Clam Gulch Inn seemed nice enough talking through his haze. People here were proud and open. And generous. Since our arrival we'd been given free of any charge fresh salmon, smoked salmon, halibut, postcards, and information—just for showing up. As far as I could tell, Alaska was just one big surprise. I expected snow here; instead, I saw interesting old junk drifted up in people's front yards waiting for a new life. I expected ostentatious trophy houses like the ones ruining the ridges of Colorado plateaus; instead I noticed people building their own modest homes with their own hands and brains. This place was like a foreign country after all. Maybe my university was right to include Alaska as a study abroad experience.

The thing I liked most about Joe's guiding style was that he didn't tell us what we would experience before we did. The day we paddled Tern Lake, Joe pushed us off two-by-two in our canoes and mentioned, almost as an afterthought, that we might see wildlife if we headed left. He didn't say that hundreds of Arctic terns were nesting over there in the bay and that they would dive bomb us within a foot of our heads if we snaked in too close through the reeds. But that's what happened. And because it did, for days the students were interested in these grey and white, fifteen-inch-long birds that migrate from Antarctica to Alaska and back each year.

As we drove over to Dwayne's place to see the huskies, Joe's hands-off style changed, and he was full of information about Dwayne: his too-quiet personality, his Iditarod victory back in the eighties. Joe told us that for years he had been a friend, not with Dwayne—who seemed more or less his same age—but with Dwayne's father, an eighty-year-old old-timer who owned and ran a big fish camp operation down on the beach and had died just a few months before the Alaska class had begun. So, even in the van something was *off*, and when I saw all those dogs and when Dwayne never shut up out there with the young women, I felt like a mother hen standing out in the Alaska cold. "Let's get out of here," I wanted to say, "make a clean get away." But I didn't.

At that point it was the puppy pen that made leaving impossible. The young women gushed over the three littlest puppies, cooing over and cradling them, and finally letting them loose to toddle around the pasture while their mother was still chained to her stake in the pen. One of the women obsessed over the puppy named Digger and insisted it looked like her. Same color dark-brown fur as her hair with the same light-brown highlights around the face. She picked Digger up and positioned his head next to hers to illustrate the comparison. She wanted to know from

Dwayne if Digger was for sale, but he didn't answer—not then. I remember that. Mostly, though, I remember the mother of the pups, a grey, wolf-like husky with glacier-blue eyes, barking and straining at her chain while her three kids wandered in the grass above one of the most beautiful bays I'd seen yet. That mother looked mean, as though she could eat me or maybe she was just worn out and cranky, her teats hanging down from so much nursing that she didn't have any choice about. Like all mothers, I thought, she needed to know she wasn't invisible, and so after five minutes or so I walked over to pet her. Even Patrick tried to entertain himself while being nice to the dogs, wrestling in the dirt with the two white adolescent pups and then standing back up with a long, shallow scratch across his cheek. After that I knew all of us, except the young women, had had enough of this place and were ready to go.

But there was Dwayne's house to the right: a modern Victorian with gables and a wraparound porch, coral colored, and huge. The elephant in the landscape. The young women picked up Digger and followed Dwayne—we all followed Dwayne—through the front door and into a floor plan where rooms oozed from one to the other, where all walls were decorated not with wildlife photographs like the interior of other houses we'd seen, but with the mounted animals themselves: bison, caribou, moose, wolf, deer, fox. Just head and neck, as if they had rammed through the walls and then stopped to pose right there in Dwayne's living room or dining room or den. That's the way the whole first level of the house was—a regular frozen zoo. Even creepier, perhaps, was the photograph of himself that Dwayne handed out to each one of us as we entered the kitchen. It was the kind of photo you might send to your friends at Christmas, only instead of children posing beside a decorated tree, Dwayne knelt in the snow with his dog team, and instead of wishing the viewer Happy Holidays from the margin, Dwayne's card announced his name, address, phone number and that he was the Iditarod champion almost twenty years ago. I tried to go with it: an Alaskan custom probably. Some kind of Iditarod protocol. But I wasn't sure.

The incident—what else can I call it—began when Dwayne reached for what I later learned was a petrified walrus penis waiting on a corner shelf and asked the young women—not me, not Joe, not Willie or Patrick—what it was and then told them. I wonder whether his answer—my God, what an answer—didn't make it to my ears or whether it was too bizarre, too unbelievable to believe, so I lost no time allowing it to dull and then disappear into my subconscious. But the young women heard him and understood his words completely—I found this out later—and they didn't look any less serene for knowing what he had said. Instead, time unfolded like art, and I was a silent audience member watching a play: Dwayne crouching in front of the first young woman; Dwayne handing her the prop; Dwayne producing his camera from the room's hot air; Dwayne delivering his big line. "Kiss it," he said, referring to the penis from the shelf, the penis cradled in the first woman's hands, "for luck." That kiss has become a picture in my mind. I can see the first woman's red lips, her shiny hair, the encounter of object and skin. And I can see Dwayne too close to his subject, the camera up against his face, his nose as long as a sled. When that scene faded, the prop was passed to the second young woman, the one with the long hair who wanted Digger, and she took it with both hands and brought it to her mouth and Dwayne was right there. And then it was woman three—with blonde hair—her hands, her lips, her eyes, like the other young women's eyes, half closed, almost coy with the camera. The whole production was smooth. It took less than a few minutes. I saw the whole thing.

◇◇◇

What I want to write is that the following day when we left for Homer, a small city on the end of the Kenai Peninsula, I immediately orchestrated a group discussion to critique our experience. Instead, no one talked about Dwayne's behavior or any of what had happened. Every so often the one young woman pined for Digger from the back seat, but the only direct acknowledgment of Dwayne I was aware of those first few days in Homer came from Joe as the two of us walked back to the van when we stopped for gas, and he mentioned, reporter-like, that Dwayne's wife had died in a Christmas Eve car accident a couple years back. A better postincident scenario than silence would have been giddy laughter. At least that way I would not have felt so alone taking out my journal and pressing the words *creep* and *jerk* and *asshole* into the paper like an adolescent who couldn't get to the essence of what she was thinking. I was angry—yes—at what this Alaskan champion had done, but I was angrier still at what I hadn't done. Usually when something goes wrong, I'm not one to hang back. I'm not that shy. There had been time for me to react as Willie and Patrick relaxed in Dwayne's leather chairs and as the young women played with Digger on Dwayne's oversized couch and as I sat noticing the loose papers on the hardwood floors and the same photograph of Dwayne's wife displayed like a redundant idea in all of the rooms. There had been time for me to mention the excessive heat in the house so that all of us were unzipping fleece jackets and pulling off what we had on underneath—the thinner jackets and sweatshirts—until we were all down to our T-shirts for this strange Sunday visit. I could have intervened when Dwayne started talking to the young women about the trip he took to Asia the previous winter and showing them pictures of bright flowers and exotic rooflines and so many women. I'm pretty sure I could have done something—anything— before Willie and Patrick fell asleep. Before I melted into the empty couch across from them. Before I realized how tired Joe looked leaning against the doorjamb with his arms crossed. Before the afternoon went haywire.

But, somehow, I did nothing that day sitting beneath Dwayne's stuffed caribou. In my defense, what could have I said as a guest of Joe's friend's son? That I didn't like his house? That all of this picture taking looked suspicious? That I thought I recognized soft-core pornography when I saw it? At the very least, I expected a quick denouement after the photo shoot, but the day just kept plowing on, dull and flat. At one point, Dwayne produced some paper and took down the three young women's addresses and told them he would ship them fresh salmon. At another point, little Digger danced and slid on the wood floor before peeing, and the women scurried to the kitchen for paper towels. I remember deciding which of two magazines parked by my left foot looked more interesting—the one about Alaska or the one about mushing—yet having time for both. That was my visible reaction to what I had witnessed: to thumb through pictures of harnessed dogs racing through snow, their eyes focused, their mouths open, all teeth and tongue.

On our fourth day in Homer, Joe took us to see exhibits in the Pratt Museum and I spent the day trying to focus on other Alaskans besides Dwayne: homesteaders north of town with their eight blond children; fishermen south, east, and west of town with their dangerous jobs; volunteers from all over the peninsula in 1989 with their mission to wash off the oil from the Exxon Valdez spill that stuck, worse than glue, to so many seabirds. The next day a water taxi dropped us off on the other side of the bay, and we talked with four trail crew guys who had just cleared the route we were planning to take. That afternoon we hiked until dinner when Joe took us to a restaurant that was all glassed in and poised over Kachemak Bay so that we were like goldfish, or maybe halibut, looking out on the world. It was then, as our pizza arrived, that I overheard Patrick and Willie joke with each other and call Dwayne "le champion," and I was jerked away from any calm I was feeling and back to that house and the memory of being under a spell.

Sometimes in life we get second chances, and to some extent, that's what I got in the restaurant when I heard that the young women had been communicating with Dwayne via cell phone ever since the incident. This news—and Dwayne's recent proposition—fell out right there on the table: according to the young women, Dwayne had invited them to go night fishing when we returned to Clam Gulch. He would pick them up at camp and bring them back the next morning. They could take showers. He would make them pancakes. They could see Digger. From the other end of the table, Joe looked at me with what had to be disbelief, and I was pretty positive then that although he'd said nothing, he had always been on my side. I could feel both of us trying to stay calm, to temper our adrenaline, to gauge the best way to go. We were, after all, the teachers, and they were the students, and even though Joe and I certainly were not in our areas of expertise, we could still encourage the group to think about the incident in a new way. At least, that's what I must have thought when I made my move and asked the students if the whole visit to Dwayne's didn't seem a little weird, a little odd, a little different than any visit they had ever taken to any house in their lives. As I framed my question, I sounded less sure than I felt. It did, of course, occur to me that I was about to take down a champ, and when all three young women looked at me with their bored lips and cataract eyes, I felt as if I were drenching them in something thick like oil. It's the feeling any teacher gets when introducing a new concept that no one wants to hear.

Not surprisingly, or so it seems to me now, the young women defended Dwayne as a good host and a star athlete and a martyr who frequently parted with his specially bred pups. "I like him," the shiny-haired woman said in too loud a voice as if it were her job to end the conversation. But somehow, I kept pushing with Joe's and even Willie's and Patrick's help, remembering details that might implicate Dwayne. The young women listened at first and then began to respond in ways that suggested they both knew and didn't know what had been going on at Dwayne's and that they both acknowledged and didn't acknowledge what we were saying. One of them insisted Dwayne was a nice man. One of them remembered the end of our visit, when

Dwayne's ex-handler came by in her short corduroy skirt and sat down close to Dwayne as if she didn't mind being near him. When I looked at the young women I saw only low voltage light bulbs going off over their heads. Even their laughter wasn't genuine. I had the sense that they saw the absurdity of the situation and understood why adults might find it alarming, but they weren't convinced that kissing anything at the request of a stranger was all that bad.

That night as I zipped myself in my tent, I already knew the Dwayne story would be the one I would tell most often when I returned to North Carolina. Of course I'd mention the bears and puffins and icebergs that rolled over as if they had been trained, but I was left with something more than a-day-late-and-a-dollar-short sensation after confronting the young women in the restaurant. As I lay in my sleeping bag, it dawned on me that even if nothing at all had happened, even if I had knocked the camera out of Dwayne's hands before the photographs were taken, even if the first woman had refused to strike her provocative pose and all of the other young women had followed her lead, I would still be lying there bothered by Dwayne himself and the way the visit to his house had ripped the fabric of my Alaska experience. Of course I didn't have it all clearly figured out that night, so it wasn't possible to slide into a sweet sleep. Like the young women who both knew and didn't know what was going on at Dwayne's, I both knew and didn't know right then that the Dwayne story, on one level, was about me. Maybe I should not have been so critical of my students' behavior.

Self-knowledge only arrives with time and work. In my case it took telling and retelling the story as a comedy before I understood the kernel embedded in the narrative that kept me from reacting to Dwayne's orchestration of events. I realized part of the truth when I was having my hair cut a few weeks after my return from Alaska so that the memory of the natural world still clashed with the surreal salon world of sinks and mirrors. Initially I thought my hairdresser might enjoy this little story from my travels, but as I sat there in my black, waterproof smock watching her reflection, as I mentioned the *Playboy* magazine I'd seen hiding beneath Dwayne's papers and the magnetic attraction Dwayne had only for those three young women, my gaze turned toward myself in the mirror, and I felt that tingling I sometimes feel when I edge close to the truth. In front of me I saw not the self that I carry around with me in my head, but a faded version of me looking out from what seemed like a slab of granite or ice. I wasn't who I once was. I had lost the power of youth for good. When I looked back at the woman who had cut my hair for fifteen years, she held my gaze with insight, and I wondered whether she figured out the most compromising and revealing details of my life because we communicated with each other through a mirror.

"It's what I hate most about getting old," she said in a way that resonated deep in my soul. "Part of us is no longer here."

∞

Our last day in Homer, I woke up before Joe did. In the distance Grewingk Glacier spread out wide and long, and I knew that giving students "The Discovery of Glacier Bay" from John Muir's *Travels in Alaska* was not that bad of an idea. Up in the common area of the campground, I filled the plastic watering can hanging in the wooden shower and peeled off four layers of clothes. Then I leaned over and baptized myself with icy water. This was what I enjoyed: physical memories of when I was a ranger wading into Roaring River after a day of patrol, more memories of when I was in my thirties bathing with my backpacking friends on the banks of whatever lake or river or spring we stopped at for the night. A shower made sweeter that morning because no one was awake, and I didn't have to justify my pleasures to the students who were waiting for real showers—warm showers—in town.

Even though we'd been camping in a farmer's field for the past three days and the students had told me about the beach, that morning was the first time I felt pulled down the grassy slope, past the roosters, past the horses, past the two square cottages without electricity that I didn't even know were there hiding in the woods. On the beach, the tide was out so that there was both sand and rocks. The sun shone without clouds. Across the bay, mountains came down and touched the waves as if they were friends. This was what was different here: ocean and mountains existed in the same eyeful. Sheets of what must have been seaweed lay rolled on the sand like parchment. Along the beach to the north, no one. To the south, no one. I walked and walked on the rocky shore, and I thought about all I'd learned the past fourteen days: the names of plants I'd never seen before, the history of Arctic gold, the expression of seals, the stories of the Inuit. And I was filled with pressurized emotion.

When I turned around, the beach was not empty. There was a figure coming toward me that, at first, I thought was one of the students, one of the women, even though at the same time I knew she wasn't. Her hair was long and straight like mine used to be, and she had on jeans. When we finally passed on the narrow part of the beach, we both smiled at each other, but we didn't stop. I knew we wouldn't, just as I knew I wouldn't reach out and touch her arm, even though something inside of me wanted to. This young woman passed me and then she was behind me, and I didn't look back. I kept walking and walking, trying not to disrupt the calm of nature, trying not to blame myself for what I had or hadn't done at Dwayne's, trying not to be embarrassed about anything on this Alaska morning. I just kept going, stepping from rock to rock and feeling as if I were connecting the dots of my life, outlining where I'd been and who I was. I remembered the little Buddhist flags I'd seen hanging in a Homer coffee shop the day before with their clear messages about what we work for in life: success, peace, tranquility, love, happiness, wisdom. Right then, for just that moment, I felt them all.

Notes

⋙ ✦ ⋘

A Portrait of My Father in Three Places

I consulted Anya Helsel, librarian at Glacier National Park.

Someone Else Dies

I consulted Charlie Logan and Larry Van Slyke, subdistrict rangers during my seven seasons working in Rocky Mountain National Park.

Death, Despair, and Second Chances in Rocky Mountain National Park by Joseph R. Evans (Boulder: Johnson Books, 2010) and *Death, Daring, and Disaster: Search and Rescue in the National Parks*, rev. ed., by Charles R. "Butch" Farabee Jr. (Lanham, MD: Taylor Trade Publishing, 2005) were also consulted.

I have changed some names in this essay.

There's an Old Dump Below Lawn Lake

Quoted material is from page 201 of Joan Didion's essay "At the Dam," published in *The White Album* (New York: Farrar, Straus, and Giroux, 1990).

Some historical information is from "A History of the North Fork Subdistrict" (unpublished), a project assigned to me by Charlie Logan, who realized that the words and lives of the people who live in and near national parks matter and need to be preserved. During the three years I worked as a backcountry ranger, I researched the subdistrict and interviewed rancher Frank McGraw, among other family members of early settlers in the region.

Backcountry Trash (and Other Important Considerations)

Some historical information is from "A History of the North Fork Subdistrict" (unpublished).

When I Leave

Kathy Brazelton, east district naturalist at Rocky Mountain National Park, was consulted about park fauna for this essay and for "Going to Die."

Going to Die

Quoted material and information about the history of mountaineering in Mount Rainier National Park is from *The Challenge of Rainier: A Record of the Explorations and Ascents, Triumphs and Tragedies, on the Northwest's Greatest Mountain*, by Dee Molenaar (Seattle: The Mountaineers, 1979). Many thanks to Brenda Bass, friend all these years, for giving me Molenaar's book at the perfect time.

Other quoted material is from John Muir's *Stickeen: The Story of a Dog* collected in *Nature Writings* (New York: Library of America, 1997) and an excerpt of a letter (unpublished) written to me by Pat Kato, my first mountain mentor, a mountain of a friend.

Mark Magnuson, chief ranger of Rocky Mountain National Park during the summer Jeff Christensen died, provided invaluable feedback on the initial draft that I constructed of the event. Mark was also consulted about park fines and the Lawn Lake flood.

I consulted Larry Van Slyke, subdistrict ranger during my years at Rocky Mountain National Park.

Death, Despair, and Second Chances by Evans and *Death, Daring, and Disaster* by Farabee Jr. were also consulted.

D.E. Glidden, field specialist in wind and mountain climatology in Rocky Mountain National Park, was consulted about wind speeds and their effects.

Thank you to Mary Metz at Mountaineers Books for permission not only to use but also to adapt the chart on Mount Rainier fatalities.

Thank you to Richard Gilbert, David Gilbert, and Mary Birdelle for giving me permission to use their mother's portrait of their uncle, Delmar Fadden, first published by Mountaineers Books in *The Challenge of Rainier: A Record of the Explorations and Ascents, Triumphs and Tragedies, on the Northwest's Greatest Mountain*. Marybeth Gilbert, their mother, was Fadden's sister.

Thank you to Gretchen Daiber and Joanne Daiber Warsinske for giving me permission to use their father's photograph of Delmar Fadden, also published in *The Challenge of Rainier*. A celebrated mountaineer, Ome Daiber, their father, led the search to rescue Fadden on Mount Rainier.

Driving to Russia
I have changed some names in this essay.

No More to the Lake
Quoted material is from pages 198, 201, and 202 of E. B. White's essay "Once More to the Lake," published in *Essays of E.B. White* (New York: Harper & Row, 1977).

Oxford Through the Looking Glass
Quoted material is from page 145 of Jan Morris's *Oxford* (Oxford: Oxford University Press, 1978).

I have changed some names in this essay.

Visiting the Iditarod Champ
I have changed some names in this essay.

CPSIA information can be obtained
at www.ICGtesting.com
Printed in the USA
BVHW041620310819
557149BV00001BA/1/P